The
ESSENTIAL COLLECTION

D1005480

Shipment Five

Rainy Day Kisses
Mail-Order Bride
The Matchmakers
Father's Day
A Friend or Two
No Competition

Shipment Six

First Comes Marriage
White Lace and Promises
Friends—and Then Some
The Way to a Man's Heart
Hasty Wedding
That Wintry Feeling
Those Christmas Angels

Shipment Seven

Borrowed Dreams
Starlight
Promise Me Forever
Shadow Chasing
For All My Tomorrows
The Playboy and the Widow

Shipment Eight

Fallen Angel
Yesterday's Hero
Reflections of Yesterday
All Things Considered
The Trouble With Caasi
Almost Paradise

The

ESSENTIAL COLLECTION

#1 *New York Times* Bestselling Author

DEBBIE
MACOMBER

Some Kind of
WONDERFUL

H HARLEQUIN® MIRA®

Recycling programs
for this product may
not exist in your area.

ISBN-13: 978-0-373-47275-8

SOME KIND OF WONDERFUL

◆ HARLEQUIN®

www.Harlequin.com

Printed in U.S.A.

DEBBIE MACOMBER

is a number one *New York Times* and *USA TODAY* best-selling author. Her books include *1225 Christmas Tree Lane*, *1105 Yakima Street*, *A Turn in the Road*, *Hannah's List* and *Debbie Macomber's Christmas Cookbook*, as well as *Twenty Wishes*, *Summer on Blossom Street* and *Call Me Mrs. Miracle*. She has become a leading voice in women's fiction worldwide and her work has appeared on every major bestseller list, including those of the *New York Times*, *USA TODAY*, *Publishers Weekly* and *Entertainment Weekly*. She is a multiple award winner, and won the 2005 Quill Award for Best Romance. There are more than one hundred million copies of her books in print. Two of her Harlequin MIRA Christmas titles have been made into Hallmark Channel Original Movies, and the Hallmark Channel has launched a series based on her bestselling Cedar Cove series. For more information on Debbie and her books, visit her website, www.debbiemacomber.com.

One

"Once upon a time in a land far away," Judy Lovin began in a still, reverent voice. The intent faces of the four-year-olds gathered at her feet stared up at her with wide-eyed curiosity. Hardly a whisper could be heard as Judy continued relating the fairy tale that had stirred her heart from the moment she'd first heard it as a youngster no older than these. It was the story of *Beauty and the Beast.*

Today, however, her thoughts weren't

on the fairy tale, which she could recite from memory. As much as she was trying to focus her attention on her job, Judy couldn't. She'd argued with her father earlier that morning and the angry exchange troubled her. She rarely disagreed with her father, a man she deeply loved and respected. Charles Lovin was an outspoken, opinionated man who headed one of the world's most successful shipping companies. At the office he was regarded as demanding but fair. At home, with his family, Charles Lovin was a kind and generous father to both Judy and her older brother, David.

Charles's Wedgwood teacup had clattered sharply when he'd placed it in the saucer that morning. "All those years of the best schooling, and you prefer to work as a preschool teacher in a day-care center." He'd said it as though she were toiling among lepers on a South Pacific island instead of the peaceful upper east side of Manhattan.

"I love what I do."

"You could have any job you wanted!" he'd snapped.

His unprovoked outburst surprised Judy and she'd answered quietly. "I have exactly the job I want."

He slapped the table, startling her. Such behavior was uncommon—indeed, unheard of—in the Lovin household. Even her brother couldn't disguise his shock.

"What good are my wealth and position to you there?" he roared. "Beauty, please..."

He used his affectionate name for her. She'd loved the fairy tale so much as a child that her father had given her the name of the princess. Today, however, she felt more like a servant than royalty. She couldn't recall a time when her father had looked at her in such a dictatorial manner. Swallowing a sip of tea, she took her time answering, hoping to divert the confrontation.

She was a gentle soul, like her mother, who had died unexpectedly when Judy was in her early teens. Father and daughter had grown close in the years that followed and even during her most rebellious teen period, Judy had hardly ever argued with him. And certainly not over something like this. When she'd graduated from the finest university in the country at the top of her class, she'd gone to work as a volunteer at a local day-care center in a poor section of town. She'd come to love her time with these preschoolers. Charles hadn't objected then, or when she'd been asked to join the staff full-time, although her pay was only a fraction of what she could make in any other job. But after all these months, it seemed unfair that her father should suddenly object.

"Father," she said, forcing herself to remain calm. "Why are you concerned about the day-care center *now?*"

He'd looked tired and drawn and so unlike himself that she'd immediately been worried.

"I'd assumed," he shouted, his expression furious, "that given time, you'd come to your senses!"

Judy attempted to disguise a smile.

"I don't find this subject the least bit amusing, young lady."

"Yes, Father."

"You have a degree from one of the finest universities in this country. I expect you to use the brain the good Lord gave you and make something of yourself."

"Yes, Father."

"Try living off what you make taking care of other women's children and see how far that gets you in this world."

She touched her mouth with her linen napkin and motioned with her head to Bently, who promptly removed her plate. The English butler had been with the family since long before Judy was born. He sent her a sympathetic look. "Do we need the money, Father?" she asked.

In retrospect, she realized she probably shouldn't have spoken in such a flippant tone. But to hear her father, it sounded as if they were about to become destitute.

Charles Lovin completely lost his temper at that, hitting the table so hard that his spoon shot into the air and hit the crystal chandelier with a loud clang, shocking them both.

"I demand that you resign today." And with that, he tossed his napkin on his plate and stormed from the room.

Judy sat for a long moment as the shock settled over her. Gradually the numbness subsided and she pushed back her genuine Queen Anne chair. All the furniture in the Lovin home had been in the family for generations. Many considered this a priceless antique; Judy considered it a dining-room chair.

Bently appeared then, a crisp linen towel folded over his forearm. He did love ceremony. "I'm sure he didn't mean that, miss." He spoke out of the corner of his mouth, barely moving his lips. It had always amused Judy that Bently could talk like that, and she assumed he'd acquired this talent from years of directing help during dinner parties and other formal gatherings.

"Thank you, Bently," she said, grinning. "I'm sure you're right."

He winked then and Judy returned the gesture. By the time she arrived at the day-care center, she'd put the thought of resigning out of her mind. Tonight when she got home, her father would be his kind, loving self again. He would apologize for his outrageous tantrum and she would willingly forgive him.

"Miss Judy, Miss Judy!" Tammi, a lively little girl, jumped to her feet and threw her arms around her teacher's neck. "That's a beautiful story."

Judy returned the wholehearted hug. "I love it, too."

"Did Beauty and the Beast love each other forever and ever?"

"Oh, yes."

"Did they have lots of little beasts?"

"I'm sure they did, but remember, the Beast wasn't a beast any longer."

"Beauty's love turned him into a handsome prince," Jennifer exclaimed, exceedingly proud of herself.

Bobby, a blond preschooler with pale

blue eyes, folded his arms across his chest and looked grim. "Do you know any stories about policemen? That's what I want to be when I grow up."

Judy affectionately ruffled the little boy's hair. "I'll see if I can find a story just for you tomorrow."

The boy gave her a wide smile and nodded his head. "Good thing. I'm tired of mushy stories."

"Now," Judy said, setting the book aside. "It's time to do some finger painting."

A chorus of cheers rose from the small group and they scurried to the tables and chairs. Judy stood up and reached over her head to the tall cupboards for the paper and paints.

"You know what I love most about the Beast?" Jennifer said, lagging behind.

"What's that?" Judy withdrew an apron from the top shelf and tied it around her waist. Her brown hair fell in soft curves, brushing her shoulders, and she pushed it back.

"I love the way Beauty brought summer into the Beast's forest."

"It was her kindness and gentleness that accomplished that," Judy reminded the little girl.

"And her love," Jennifer added, sighing.

"And her love," Judy repeated.

"I have the report you requested."

John McFarland glanced up from the accounting sheets he was studying. "Put it here." He pointed to the corner of his beech desk and waited until his business manager, Avery Anderson, had left the room before reaching for the folder.

McFarland opened it, stared at the picture of the lovely brown-eyed woman that rested on top and arched his brows appreciatively. Judy Lovin. He'd seen her picture in the *New York Times* several months ago, but the photo hadn't done her fragile beauty justice. As he recalled, the article had described her efforts in a day-care center. He studied her photograph. Although she was lovely, he knew women who were far more beautiful. However, few of them revealed such trusting innocence and subtle grace. The women he dealt with all had a seductive beauty, but lacked heart. Seeing Judy's photograph, McFarland was struck anew at the contrast.

He continued to stare at the picture. Her dark brown eyes smiled back at him and McFarland wondered if she had half the backbone her father possessed. The thought of the man caused his mouth to tighten with an odd mixture of admiration and displeasure. He had liked Charles Lovin when he'd first met him; he'd been openly challenged by him several years later. Few men had the courage to tangle with McFarland, but the older man was stubborn, tenacious, ill-tempered…and, unfortunately, a fool. A pity, McFarland mused, that anyone would allow pride to stand in the way of common sense. The U.S. shipping business had been swiftly losing ground for decades. Others had seen it and diversified or sold out. If McFarland hadn't bought them outright, he'd taken control by other channels. Charles Lovin, and only Lovin, had steadfastly refused to relinquish his business—to his own detriment, McFarland mused. Apparently, leaving a dying company to his beloved son, David, was more important than giving him nothing.

Lovin was the last holdout. The others had crumpled easily enough, giving in when McFarland had applied pressure in varying degrees. Miraculously, Lovin had managed to hang on to his company. Word was that he'd been cashing in stocks, bonds and anything else he could liquidate. Next, he supposed, it would be priceless family heirlooms. It was a shame, but he felt little sympathy. McFarland was determined to own Lovin Shipping Lines and one stubborn old man wouldn't stand in his way. It was a pity, though; Lovin had guts and despite everything, McFarland admired the man's tenacity.

Leafing through the report, he noted that Lovin had managed to get a sizable loan from a New York bank. Satisfied, McFarland nodded and his lips twisted with wry humor. He was a major stockholder of that financial institution and several other Manhattan banks, as well. He pushed the buzzer on his desk and Avery appeared, standing stiffly in front of him.

"You called, sir?"

"Sit down, Avery." McFarland gestured to an imposing leather wing chair. Avery had been with McFarland four years and John had come to respect the other man's keen mind.

"Did you read the report?"

"Yes."

McFarland nodded and absently flipped through the pages.

"David Lovin is well thought of in New York," Avery added. "He's serious and hardworking. Wealth doesn't appear to have spoiled the Lovin children."

"David?" McFarland repeated, surprised that he'd been so preoccupied that he'd missed something.

"The young man who will inherit the Lovin fortune."

"Yes, of course." McFarland had examined the Lovin girl's photograph and been so taken with her that he hadn't gone on to read the report on her older brother. He did so now and was impressed with the young man's credentials.

"Many people believe that if Lovin Shipping Lines can hold on for another year…"

"Yes, yes." McFarland knew all that. Congress was said to be considering new laws that would aid the faltering shipping business. McFarland was counting on the same legislation himself.

"Father and son are doing everything possible to manage until Washington makes a move."

"It's a shame," McFarland murmured almost inaudibly.

"What's a shame?" Avery leaned forward.

"To call in his loan."

"You're going to do it?"

McFarland studied his employee,

astonished that the other man would openly reveal his disapproval. John knew that to all the world, he seemed to be a man without conscience, without scruples, without compassion. He *was* all those things—and none of them. John McFarland was an entity unto himself. People didn't know him because he refused to let anyone get close. He had his faults, he'd be the first to admit that, but he'd never cheated anyone.

He stood abruptly, placed his hands behind his back and paced the area in front of his desk. David Lovin was a fortunate man to have a heritage so richly blessed; McFarland knew nothing of his own family. Orphaned at an early age, he'd been given up for adoption. No family had ever wanted him and he'd been raised in a series of foster homes—some better than others.

McFarland had clawed his way to

the top an inch at a time. He'd gotten a scholarship to college, started his first company at twenty-one and been a millionaire by twenty-five. At thirty-six, he was one of the wealthiest men in the world. Surprisingly, money meant little to him. He enjoyed the riches he'd accumulated, the island, his home, his Learjet; money brought him whatever he desired. But wealth and position were only the by-products of success. Unlike those whose fortunes had created—or were created by—family businesses, McFarland's empire would die with him. The thought was a sobering one. Money had given him everything he'd ever wanted except what he yearned for most—love, acceptance, self-worth. A paradox, he realized somewhat sadly. Over the years, he'd grown hard. Bitter. Everything in him demanded that he topple Lovin as he had a hundred other businesses. Without sentiment or regret. The only thing stopping him was that damnable pride he'd recognized in Charles Lovin's eyes. The man was a fighter and he hated to take him down without giving the old boy a chance.

"Sir, do you wish to think this matter through?"

McFarland had nearly forgotten Avery's presence. He nodded abruptly and the other man quietly left the room.

Opening the doors that led to the veranda, McFarland stepped outside, leaned on the wrought-iron railing and looked out on the clear blue waves crashing against the shore far below. He'd purchased this Caribbean island three years earlier and named it St. Steven's. It granted him privacy and security. Several families still inhabited the far side of the island, and McFarland allowed them to continue living there. They tended to avoid him, and on the rare occasions he happened to meet any of them, they slipped quickly away.

A brisk wind blew off the water, carrying with it the scent of seaweed, and he tasted salt on his tongue. Farther down the beach, he saw a lazy trail of foam that had left its mark on the sand, meandering without purpose into the distance. Sometimes that was the way McFarland viewed his life; he was without inner purpose and yet on the surface, his activities were dominated by it. Another paradox, he mused, not unhappily, not really caring.

Unexpectedly, he made a decision and returned to his desk, again ringing for his assistant.

Avery was punctual as usual. "Sir?"

McFarland sat in his chair and rocked back, fingering his chin. "I've decided."

Avery nodded, reaching for his paper and pen.

McFarland hesitated. "I wonder how much that business means to the old man."

"By all accounts—everything."

McFarland grinned. "Then we shall see."

"Sir?"

"Contact Lovin as soon as possible and give him an ultimatum. Either I'll call in the loan—immediately—or he sends me his daughter." He picked up the file. "I believe her name is Judy.... Yes, here it is. Judy."

Avery's pad dropped to the carpet. Flustered, he bent to retrieve the paper, and in the process lost his pen, which rolled under McFarland's desk. Hastily, he rescued them both and, with nervous, jerky movements, reclaimed his place. "Sir, I think I misunderstood you."

"Your hearing is fine."

"But…sir?"

"Naturally there will be a number of guarantees on my part. We can discuss those at a later date."

"Sir, such a…why, it's unheard of—I mean, no man in his right mind—"

"I agree it's a bit unorthodox."

"A…bit? But surely…sir?" Avery stuttered.

Watching, McFarland found him highly amusing. The man had turned three shades of red, each deeper than the one before. A full minute passed and he'd opened his mouth twice, closed it an equal number of times and opened it again. Yet he said nothing.

"What about the young lady? She may have a few objections," Avery finally managed.

"I'm confident that she will."

"But…"

"We'll keep her busy with whatever

it is women like to do. I suppose she could redecorate the downstairs. When I tire of her, I'll set her free. Don't look so concerned, Avery. I've yet to allow my baser instincts to control me."

"Sir, I didn't mean to imply...it's just that..."

"I understand." McFarland was growing bored with this. "Let me know when he gives you his decision."

"Right away, sir." But he looked as if he would've preferred a trip to the dentist.

Judy returned home from work that afternoon, weary in both body and spirit. She smiled at Bently, who took her coat and purse.

"Is my father home?" Judy asked, eager to settle this matter between them. If he felt as strongly as he had that morning about her job at the day care, then she'd do as he requested.

"Mr. Lovin is still at the office, Miss Judy."

Judy checked her watch, surprised that her father was this late. He was almost always home an hour or so before her. "I'll wait for him in the study," Judy said. Something was worrying him; Judy was positive. Whatever the problem was, Judy yearned to assure him that she'd help in any way possible. If it meant leaving the daycare center then she would, but she was happy working with the children. Surely he wanted her happiness. Being a success shouldn't be judged by how much money one happened to make. Contentment was the most important factor, and she was sure that someone as wise and considerate as her father would agree.

"In the study, miss? Very good. Shall I bring you tea?"

"That would be lovely. Thank you."

He bowed slightly and turned away.

Judy entered the library, which was connected to her father's study by huge sliding doors. She chose to wait among the leather-bound volumes and settled into the soft armchair, slipped off her pumps and rested her feet on the ottoman, crossing them at the ankles. The portrait of her mother, hanging over the marble fireplace, smiled down on her. Judy would sometimes sneak into the room and talk with her mother. On occasion, she could've sworn Georgia's eyes had moved. That was silly, of course, and Judy had long ago accepted that her mother was gone and the portrait was exactly that—a likeness of a lovely woman and nothing more.

Judy stared up at her now. "I can't imagine what got into Father this morning."

The soft, loving eyes appeared to caress Judy and plead with her to be patient.

"I've never known him to be in such an unreasonable and foul mood."

Her mother's look asked her to be more understanding and Judy quickly glanced away. "All right, all right," she grumbled. "I'll be more patient."

Bently came into the study, carrying a silver tray. "Shall I pour?"

"I'll do it," she answered with a smile. She reached for the pot. "Bently?"

"Yes, miss?" He turned back to her.

"Whatever happened to the Riordan sculpture that was on Father's desk?" The small bronze statue was a prized piece that her father had always loved.

"I…don't really know, miss."

"Did Father move it to his office?"

"That must be it."

"He'd never sell it." Judy was convinced of that. The Alice Riordan original had been a Christmas gift from her mother a few months before she died.

"I'm sure he didn't," the butler concurred and then excused himself.

Now that she considered it, she realized there were other things missing from the house—a vase here and there, a painting that had disappeared. Judy hadn't given the matter much thought, but now she found it odd. Either her father had moved them to another location for safekeeping or they'd simply vanished into thin air. Even to entertain the notion that the staff would steal them was unthinkable. Bently, Cook and Anne had been with the Lovins for years.

Judy poured her tea and added a squeeze of fresh lemon. Bently had been thoughtful enough to bring two extra cups so that when her father and

David arrived, they could have tea, as well.

She must have drifted off to sleep because the next thing Judy heard was the sound of gruff male voices. The door between the two rooms had been closed, but she could hear the raised impatient voices of her father and brother as clearly as if they were in the library with her.

Judy sat upright and rubbed the stiffness from the back of her neck. She was about to interrupt her father and brother and cajole them into a cup of tea, but something held her back. Perhaps it was the emotion she recognized in their voices—the anger, the outrage, the frustration. Judy paid little attention to the business; that was her brother and father's domain. But it was apparent that something was dreadfully wrong.

"You can't mean you actually sold

the Riordan?" David's astonished voice echoed off the paneled walls.

"Do you think I wanted to?" Charles Lovin said, and the agony in his voice nearly caused her heart to stop. "I was desperate for the money."

"But, Father—"

"You can't say anything to me that I haven't told myself a thousand times."

"What else?" David sounded worried and grim.

"Everything I could."

The announcement was followed by a shocked gasp, but Judy didn't know if it had come from her throat or her brother's.

"Everything?" David repeated, his voice choked.

"As much as possible without losing this house…and it still wasn't enough."

"What about Bently and the others?"

"They'll have to be let go."

"But, Father—"

"There's no other way," he cried. "As it is, we're still millions short."

Judy didn't know what was happening, but this had to be a nightmare. Reality could never be this cruel. Her father was selling everything they owned? In addition to this estate, they owned homes all over the world. There were securities, bonds, properties, investments.... Their family wealth went back for generations.

A fist slammed against the desk. "Why would McFarland call in the loan?"

"Who knows why that beast would do anything? He's ruined better men than me."

"For what reason?"

Her father paused. "Perhaps he enjoys it. God knows, I've been enough of a challenge for him. From what I've been able to learn about the man, he has no conscience. He's a nobody," he said bitterly. The next words were smothered, as though her father had buried his face in his hands. "...something I didn't tell you...something you should know...McFarland wants our Beauty."

"What?" David shouted.

Judy bolted upright, her back rigid. It was apparent that they weren't aware she was in the other room.

"I heard from his business manager today. Avery Anderson spoke for McFarland and stated that either we come up with the amount of the loan plus the accumulated interest or send Judy to St. Steven's."

"St. Steven's?"

"That's the name of his private island."

"What does he want with...her?"

"Only God knows." The suffering in her father's voice ripped at Judy's heart. "He swears he won't abuse her in any way, and that she'll have free run of the island, but..."

"Oh, Dad." David must have slumped into a chair. "So you had to decide between a business that's been in our family for four generations and your daughter?"

"Those were exactly my choices."

"What...did you tell him?"

"You don't want to hear what I said to that man."

"No," David whispered, "I don't suppose I do."

"We have no option," Charles Lovin said through gritted teeth. "McFarland wins. I won't have Judy subjected to that beast." Despair weighed down his words.

Numb, her whole body trembling, Judy leaned back in the chair. Lovingly she ran her hand over the soft brown leather. This chair, like so much of what they owned, had been part of a heritage that had been in their family for generations. Soon it would all be lost to them.

And only she could prevent it from happening.

Two

Judy's hand tightened around the suitcase handle as she stood on the deserted dock. The powerboat that had brought her to St. Steven's roared away behind her. She refused to look back, afraid that if she did, her courage would abandon her.

The island was a tropical paradise—blue skies, soft breezes, pristine beaches and crystal clear water. Huge palm trees bordered the beach, swaying gently. The scent of magnolias and orchids wafted invitingly toward her.

A tall man Judy guessed to be in his late forties approached her. He wore a crisp black suit that revealed the width of his muscular shoulders. His steps made deep indentations in the wet sand.

She'd only brought one suitcase, packing light with the prayer that her stay would be a brief one. The single piece of luggage now felt ten times heavier than when she'd left New York that morning.

Her father had driven her to the airport, where McFarland's private jet was waiting to take her to a secluded airstrip. From there, she was told, it would be a short boat trip to the island. Tears had glistened in her father's faded blue eyes. He'd hardly spoken and when the moment came for Judy to leave, he'd hugged her so tightly she hadn't been able to breathe.

"Goodbye, Judy." His whispered

words had been strangled by emotion. "If he hurts you…"

"He won't," she assured him. "I'll be fine—and back home so soon you won't even know I've been gone."

A pinched look had come over his face and he'd whispered, "I'll know. Every minute you're away, I'll know."

Leaving her family hadn't been easy for Judy, especially when she felt as though she was being ripped from their arms.

After innocently eavesdropping on her father and David's conversation, Judy had openly confronted them. She would go to McFarland and they could do nothing to stop her. Her stubborn determination had stunned them both. But she'd refused to hear their arguments and had simply gone about packing. Within twenty-four hours she was on her way to St. Steven's.

She was here now, outwardly calm

and mentally prepared to do whatever she must.

"Ms. Lovin?" the man asked politely, meeting her at the end of the pier.

Judy nodded, momentarily unable to find her voice.

"We've been expecting you." He reached for her suitcase, taking it from her hand. "Come with me, please."

Judy followed the stranger. He led her into the nearby trees to a cart that reminded her of something she'd seen on the golf course. Only this one was far more powerful and surged ahead at the turn of a key.

When they came upon the house, Judy's breath was trapped in her lungs. It was the most magnificent place she'd ever seen. Built on the edge of a cliff, it was nestled in foliage and adorned with pillars and balconies. Tropical vines climbed the exterior walls, twisting upward.

"This way," the man said, standing on the walkway that led into the grand house.

Judy climbed out of the cart and followed him through the massive doors. In the marble entryway she was met by a short, thin man. She identified him immediately as McFarland's assistant, the man she'd heard her father mention. He looked like an Avery, she thought—efficient, intelligent…bookish.

"Ms. Lovin," he greeted her with an embarrassed smile. "I trust your journey was a pleasant one."

"Most pleasant." She returned his smile, although her knees felt like tapioca pudding. "You must be Mr. Anderson."

If he was surprised that she knew his name, he didn't reveal it. "Your rooms are ready if you'd like to freshen up before dinner."

"Please."

He rang a bell and a maid appeared as though by magic. The woman's gaze didn't meet Judy's as she silently escorted her up the stairs. The maid held open a pair of double doors, and Judy walked into a parlorlike room complete with fireplace, television, bookshelves and two sofas. Off the parlor was a bedroom so lovely Judy stared in amazement at the elegant pastel colors. The view of the ocean from the balcony was magnificent. She stood at the railing, the wind whipping her hair about her face, and saw a swimming pool and a tennis court. To her far right, she located another building that she assumed must be the stables. Her heart gladdened. She'd been riding almost from the time she could walk and loved horses. Her cage was indeed a gilded one.

"Dinner will be in fifteen minutes," the maid informed her.

"Thank you," Judy responded. She squared her shoulders and her heart pounded faster. Soon she'd be meeting the infamous McFarland—the man her father called the Beast.

But Judy was wrong. When she descended the stairs, armed with questions to which she was determined to find answers, she learned to her dismay that she'd be dining alone.

Mr. Anderson lived in a small house on the island and had departed for the day. McFarland had sent his regrets, but business prevailed. His brief note indicated that he was looking forward to meeting her in the morning.

The dining-room table was set for eight with a service of the finest bone china. The butler seated Judy at one end. The servants brought in course after course, their footsteps echoing in the silent room. Each course was delectable, but Judy ate little. Afterward, she returned to her room.

Her sleep was fitful as questions interrupted her dreams. She wondered if McFarland was playing some kind of psychological game meant to intimidate her. If he was, then she'd fallen an unwilling victim to it. She didn't know much about John McFarland. He was rarely if ever seen in public and she'd been unable to locate any photos of him on any Internet site. Her father insisted he was arrogant, impudent, insolent, unorthodox and perhaps the worst insult—beastly.

What a strange place this was, she thought tiredly, staring up at the darkened ceiling. The house was built in a paradise of sun and sea and yet a chill pervaded her bones.

By six, she couldn't bear to stay in bed any longer. Throwing back the covers, she rose and decided to head for the stables. She yearned to ride, to exorcise the fears that plagued her.

The house was like a tomb—silent, dark, somber—as Judy crept down the stairs. The front door opened easily and she slipped outside. The sun was rising, cloaking the island in golden threads of light.

At a noise behind her she twisted around. A stranger on horseback was approaching her slowly. Even from a distance, Judy noticed that he sat tall and straight in the saddle. He wore a cowboy hat pulled low over his eyes.

She hesitated. No doubt he was a security guard and from the way he regarded her, he was either looking for trouble or expecting it.

"Good morning," she called out tentatively.

He touched the brim of his hat in

greeting. "Is there a problem?" His voice was deep and resonant.

"A...problem? No, of course not."

His finely shaped mouth curved with amusement as he studied her from head to foot.

Not knowing what else to do, Judy returned his look, staring into those compelling blue eyes. She thought for a moment that he was silently laughing at her and she clenched her fists. Hot color climbed up her neck, invading her cheeks. "It's a beautiful morning."

"Were you thinking of going for a walk?" He shifted his weight in the saddle and at the sound of creaking leather, Judy realized that he was dismounting. He took a step toward her.

Before she could stop herself, Judy stepped back in retreat. "No...I was going to the stables. McFarland said I could go anyplace I wanted on the island and...I thought I'd have someone choose a horse for me. Of course, I could saddle it myself."

Bold blue eyes looked straight into hers. "I frighten you?"

"No…that's ridiculous." She felt like a stuttering fool. He didn't frighten her as much as he enthralled her. He radiated a dark energy with his brooding eyes and tall, lean build.

He grinned at her response and the movement crinkled the lines around his eyes and creased his bronze cheeks. "Relax, I'm not going to pounce on you."

She stiffened. "I didn't think you would." Surely the help respected Mc-Farland's guests—if she could call herself that.

"I'll walk you to the stables." He reached for the reins and the huge black horse followed obediently behind.

"Have you been on the island long?"

she managed shakily, and attempted to smile.

"Three years."

She nodded, clasping her hands tightly in front of her. This was the first person she'd had the opportunity to speak with and she wanted to find out as much as she could about McFarland before actually meeting him. In her mind she'd conjured up several pictures, none of them pleasant. She knew he had to be an unhappy, lonely man. Old, decrepit, cantankerous. "What's he like?"

"Who?"

"McFarland."

A muscle worked in his lean jaw and when he looked at her again, his eyes were dark and enigmatic. "Some say he's a man without a heart."

Judy grinned and lowered her own eyes to the ground. "My father calls him the Beast."

"The Beast." He seemed to find that

amusing. "Some claim there's no compassion in him. Others say he has no conscience."

She glanced at the man's lathered, dusty horse and then at him. Pride showed in the tilt of his strong chin and the set of his shoulders. Thoughtfully, she shook her head. "No," she said slowly, "I don't agree with that."

"You don't?"

"No," she repeated confidently. "He appreciates beauty too much. And if he didn't have a conscience he would've—" She realized she was saying much more than she should to one of McFarland's employees. McFarland could have ruined her father ten times over, but hadn't. He might not have a heart of gold, but he wasn't without conscience. Nor was he cruel.

"What do *you* think he's like? I take it you haven't met the man."

"I'm not sure how I feel about him.

As you say, we haven't met, but from what I've seen, I'd guess there's precious little joy in his life."

The man laughed outright. "Look around you," he said. "He's said to be one of the richest men in the world. How could any man have so much and not be happy?"

"Joy comes from within," she explained. "There's too much bitterness in him. He obviously hasn't experienced true contentment."

"And who are you? A psychiatrist?"

It was Judy's turn to laugh; she'd grown more at ease with this dark stranger. "No. I formed my opinions before I came to the island."

"Wait until you meet him, then. You may be pleasantly surprised."

"Perhaps." But Judy doubted it.

They arrived at the stables and were met by a burly older man, who ambled out.

"Good morning, Sam."

"Morning," the other man grumbled, eyeing Judy curiously.

"Saddle Princess for Ms. Lovin and see to it that Midnight gets extra oats. He deserves it after the ride I gave him this morning."

Judy turned abruptly. "How did you know my name?"

He ignored her, but his eyes softened slightly at her questioning look. "Tomorrow morning, saddle both horses at five-thirty. Ms. Lovin and I will be riding together."

"Consider it done, Mr. McFarland."

Embarrassment washed over Judy. She dared not look at him.

"I'll see you at lunch, Ms. Lovin."

It was all she could do to nod.

The morning passed with surprising speed. Judy hadn't ridden in months and her body was unaccustomed to the rigors of the saddle. She hadn't gone far, preferring to investigate the island another day. A hot breakfast awaited her after she'd showered and she ate eagerly. When she'd finished, she had written her father a long letter. She'd been told that no direct contact—like phone calls or e-mail messages— would be allowed; letters were permitted, however, and would be mailed for her. Once she'd completed and addressed the letter, she lay back on the velvet sofa and closed her eyes, listening to music. The balcony doors were open and the fresh sea air swirled around her.

Someone knocked politely at her door. A maid had been sent to inform Judy that lunch would be served in ten minutes.

Experiencing dread and excitement at once, Judy stood, repaired the damage to her hair and makeup and slowly descended the stairs. She paused at the bottom, gathered her resolve and forced a smile, wondering how long it would last. She didn't expect to maintain the cheerful facade, but it was important to give McFarland the impression that she'd been unruffled by their earlier encounter. Her palms were already damp in anticipation of the second meeting with the man who ruled an empire from this island.

He stood when she entered the dining room.

"I trust your morning was satisfactory," he said.

Boldly, Judy met his probing gaze. "Why am I here?" She hadn't meant to immediately hurl questions at him, but his discerning look had unnerved her.

"I believe it's to eat lunch. Please sit down, Ms. Lovin. I, for one, am hungry, and our meal will be served as soon as you're comfortable."

The butler held out a mahogany chair at the end of the table, where she'd eaten the night before. With rebellion boiling in her blood, Judy sat on the brocade cushion.

A bowl of consommé was set in front of her. When Judy lifted her spoon, she discovered that her hand was trembling and she tightened her grip.

"How long do you plan to keep me here?" she asked. Six place settings separated them; the distance could've been far greater for all the notice McFarland gave her.

"You'll be free to go shortly," he announced between courses, having waited a full five minutes before responding.

"I can leave?" she said in astonishment. "When?"

"Soon." He gauged her expression grimly. "Are you so miserable?"

"No," she admitted, smoothing the

linen napkin across her lap. "The island is lovely."

"Good." His eyes grew gentle.

"Whose decision was it for you to come?" he asked unexpectedly.

"Mine."

He nodded and seemed to approve. "I imagine that your father and brother were opposed to your willingness to sacrifice yourself." He said this with more than a hint of sarcasm.

"Adamantly. I probably never would've been told of your...ultimatum, but I accidentally overheard them discussing it."

"You were wise to come."

"How's that?"

"I wouldn't have hesitated to call in the loan."

"I don't doubt that for a second," she said, disliking him. Her fingers gripped the napkin in her lap, but that was the only outward sign of anger that she allowed herself.

His grin lacked humor. "If you'd refused, you would've been burdened with a terrible guilt. In time, your peace and happiness would have been affected."

The butler took away her untouched salad and served the main course. Judy stared down at the thin slices of roast beef, smothered in gravy and mushrooms, and knew she wouldn't be able to eat.

"Have you always been this dictatorial?" Judy demanded.

"Always." He carefully sliced his meat.

She thought of the class of four-year-olds she'd left behind. "You must have been a difficult child." His teen years didn't bear contemplating.

Slowly, deliberately, McFarland lowered his knife and fork to the table. His eyes were sad. "I was never a child."

Princess was saddled and ready for her early the following morning. Judy patted the horse's nose and produced a carrot from the hip pocket of her jeans.

"At great personal danger, I sneaked into the kitchen and got you this," she whispered, running her hand down the mare's brown face. "Now, don't you dare tell Sam, or he'll be mad at me." Judy had quickly realized that Sam ruled the stables like his own castle and she could well be stepping on the older man's toes.

"Do you have something for me, as well?" The deep male voice spoke from behind her.

Judy whirled around to see McFarland. "No," she said, shaking her head. "I hope you don't mind…" She eyed the rapidly disappearing carrot.

He was dressed in black this morning, his expression brooding. Once again his hat brim shadowed his face. His mood seemed as dark and dangerous as his clothes. "You needn't worry about stealing vegetables."

Without another word, he mounted his horse with supple ease. He hesitated long enough to reach for the reins and sent Judy a look that said she was welcome to join him or go her own way.

Quickly, Judy placed her foot in the stirrup and swung onto Princess's back, grabbed the reins and cantered after him.

McFarland rode at an unrelenting gallop, leading her into the jungle. The footpath was narrow and steep. Birds cawed angrily and flew out of their way, their wings beating against the underbrush. Leaves and branches slapped at Judy's face; mud spattered her boots and jeans. Still he didn't lessen his furious pace. It took all of Judy's skill just to keep up with him. She barely managed. By the time he slowed, she was winded and her muscles ached. He directed Midnight onto the beach and Judy followed gratefully, allowing Princess to trot along the sandy shoreline.

Judy stared at him. Panting, she was too breathless to speak coherently. "Good—grief, McFarland—do you always tear—through the jungle like that?"

"No." He didn't look at her. "I wanted to see how well you ride."

"And?"

"Admirably well." He grinned, and his eyes sparkled with humor. Judy found herself involuntarily returning his smile.

"Next time," she said between gasps, "*I* choose the route." Dark mud dotted her clothes and face. Her hair fell in wet tendrils around her cheeks and she felt as though they'd galloped through a swamp.

He, on the other hand, had hardly splattered his shiny boots.

"Tell me about Judy Lovin," he demanded unexpectedly as they trotted side by side.

"On one condition. I want you to answer something for me."

"One question?"

"Only one," she promised, raising her right hand as though swearing an oath.

"All right."

"What do you want to know?"

"Details."

She nodded curtly. "I weighed just under seven pounds when I was born—"

"Perhaps current information would be more appropriate," he cut in.

Judy threw back her head and laughed. "Fine. I'm twenty-six—"

"That old?"

She glowered at him. "How am I supposed to tell you anything if you keep interrupting?"

"Go on."

"Thank you," she muttered sarcastically. "Let me see—I suppose you want the vitals. I'm five-five, which is short, I know, and I weigh about... No." She shook her head. "I don't think that's information a woman should share with a man."

He chuckled and Judy drew back on the reins, surprised at the deep rich sound. She suspected he didn't often give in to the urge.

He sent her an odd, half-accusing look. "Is something wrong?"

"No," she responded, feeling self-conscious. He really should laugh more often, she thought. He looked young and carefree and less—she couldn't find the word—*driven,* she decided.

"What about men?"

"Men?"

"As in beaux, boyfriends, dates, male companionship—that kind of thing."

"I date frequently." Although that was a slight misrepresentation of the truth...

"Anyone special?"

"No—unless you consider Bobby. He's four and could steal my heart with a pout." She stopped Princess, swung her leg over the horse's back and slowly lowered her feet to the ground.

McFarland dismounted, as well.

"My turn."

He shrugged. "Fire away."

"May I call you by your name?" She found it ridiculous that a man would be called simply McFarland.

"My name? You mean my first name?"

"Yes."

He hesitated long enough for her to become uneasy. Then he nodded.

"Thank you." She dropped her gaze to her mud-coated boots. "John," she whispered.

"Well?" he prompted. "Do you think it suits me?"

"It does," she told him.

"I'm glad to hear it," he said, and she wasn't sure whether he was mocking her. Then she decided it didn't matter if he was.

"You really aren't a beast, are you?" she murmured.

He frowned at that and brushed a wet strand of hair from her cheek. His fingers trailed across her face, causing her stomach to lurch at the unexpected contact.

"But you, my dear, are a Beauty."

Judy went cold. "How did you know my father called me that?"

"I know everything about you. Right down to that wimp you thought you were in love with a couple of years back. What was his name again? Richard. Yes, Richard. I'm also aware that you've rarely dated since—disillusionment, I suppose."

Judy felt the blood drain from her face.

"I know you fancy yourself a savior to that group of four-year-olds. How noble of you to squander yourself on their behalf, but I doubt they appreciate it." His blue eyes were as cold as glacial ice.

Judy thought she might be sick.

He waited, his expression filled with grim amusement. "What, no comment?"

"None." She threw the reins over Princess's head. "Thank you for the ride, John. It was quite exhilarating." Her chin held at a proud angle, she mounted and silently rode away, her back rigid.

McFarland watched her go and slammed his boot viciously against the sand. He didn't know what had made him speak to her like that. He'd known from the moment he'd seen her picture that she was like no other woman he'd ever encountered. Another woman would have thrown angry words at him for the unprovoked attack. Judy hadn't. She'd revealed courage and grace, a rare combination. McFarland didn't think he'd seen the two qualities exemplified so beautifully in any one woman. Most were interested in his wealth and power.

He didn't like the feelings Judy Lovin aroused in him. Studying her picture was one thing, but being close to her, feeling the energy she exuded, watching her overcome her natural reserve, had all greatly affected him.

Judy was good—too good for him. As other people said, he chewed up little girls like her and spit them out. He didn't want to see that happen to Judy.

What an odd position to be in, he mused darkly. He had to protect her from himself.

Three

Princess's hind feet kicked up sand as Judy trotted her along the beach. Her thoughts were in turmoil. What a strange, complex man John McFarland was. His eyes had been gentle and kind, almost laughing, when he'd asked her to tell him about herself, and yet he'd obviously known everything there was to know. Her cheeks burned with humiliation that he'd discovered what a fool she'd made of herself over Richard. She'd been so trusting, so guileless with her affection and her heart—so agonizingly stupid to have fallen in love with a married man. The pain of Richard's deception no longer hurt Judy, but her own flagrant stupidity continued to embarrass her.

Judy was so caught up in her memories that she didn't notice the children at first. Their laughter drifted on the cool morning air and she drew in her reins. As always, the mare responded instantly to Judy's signal.

"Princess, look," she said excitedly. "Children." They were playing a game of hide-and-seek, darting in and out of the jungle and rushing to the water's edge. Judy counted seven children between the ages of eight and twelve, from what she could guess.

They didn't seem to notice her, which was just as well since she didn't want to disturb their game. The smallest, a boy, had apparently been chosen as "it" and the others scattered, smothering their laughter as they ran across the sand.

Judy swung out of the saddle.

Her action must have drawn their attention because the laughter stopped abruptly. She turned around to find all the youngsters running to hide. Only the one small boy remained.

Judy smiled. "Good morning," she said cautiously, trying not to frighten him.

He was silent, his deep brown eyes serious and intense.

Digging in the pocket of her jodhpurs, Judy pulled out two sugar cubes. The first she fed to Princess. The second she held out to the boy.

He eyed it for a long time before stepping forward and grabbing it from her hand. Quickly, he jumped away from her. Holding it in his own palm, he carefully approached the horse. When

Princess lowered her sleek head and ate the cube from his hand, he looked up and grinned broadly at Judy.

"She's very gentle," Judy said softly. "Would you like to sit in the saddle?"

He nodded enthusiastically and Judy helped him mount.

Astride Princess, the boy placed both hands on the saddle and sat up straight, as though he were a king surveying his kingdom. Gradually, the other children came out from their hiding places among the trees.

"Good morning," Judy greeted each one. "My name is Judy."

"Peter."

"Jimmy."

"Philippe."

"Elizabeth."

"Margaret."

They all rushed toward her, eager to be her friend and perhaps get the chance to sit on her beautiful horse.

Judy threw up her hands and laughed. "One at a time, or I'll never be able to remember." She laid her hand on the slim shoulder of one of the younger girls. "I'm pleased to make your acquaintance." She was rewarded with a toothless smile.

From a ridge high above the beach, McFarland looked down on the scene below, a silent witness to Judy's considerable charm. She was a natural with children, and although he shouldn't be surprised at the way they gravitated toward her, he was. More often than he could count, he'd come upon the island children playing in the surf or along the beach. Usually he saw little more than a fleeting glimpse of one or two running away as though they were afraid of him.

Until he'd watched Judy enchant these children, McFarland hadn't given a second thought to the few families who made this island their home. He allowed them to remain on St. Steven's, not for any humanitarian reason, but simply because his feeling toward them was one of indifference. They could stay or leave as they wished.

Unfortunately, he couldn't say the same about Judy Lovin. The sound of her laughter swirled around him. As he watched her now with these children, an unwilling smile touched his mouth. He, too, was a victim of the enchantment she'd brought to his island.

And he didn't like it, not one damn bit.

Pulling back sharply on Midnight's reins, McFarland turned the horse and rode toward the other side of the island as if the fires of hell were licking at their heels.

By the time Judy returned to the house, McFarland had already eaten breakfast and sequestered himself in his office. Judy wasn't disappointed. She'd purposely stayed away in an effort to avoid clashing with him a second time that morning. The man puzzled her and she didn't know how to react to him.

Feeling increasingly unsettled as morning turned to midday, she ordered a light lunch and ate in her room. In the afternoon, she swam in the Olympic-size pool, forcing herself to swim lap after lap as she worked out her confusion and frustration. She had no clue as to why McFarland had sent for her other than to torment her family, and she hated to think he'd purposely do that. If she'd understood him better, she might be able to discern his motives.

Breathless from the workout, Judy climbed out of the pool and reached for her towel, burying her face in its plush thickness. As she drew it over her arms and legs, goose bumps prickled her skin and she realized she was being watched. A chill shivered up her spine and she paused to glance around. She could see no one, but the feeling persisted and she hurriedly gathered her things.

In her own rooms, Judy paced, uncertain and unsettled. Eventually she sat down at the large desk and wrote another long, chatty letter to her father and brother. The hallway was silent when she came out of her room. She hesitated only a moment before making her way downstairs and into the wing of the house from where she suspected McFarland ruled his empire.

"Ms. Lovin?"

Avery Anderson's voice stopped her short when she turned a corner and happened upon a large foyer. "Hello," she said with feigned brightness. "I apologize if I'm intruding."

Avery stood, his hands on the top of his desk as he leaned forward. "It's no intrusion," he said, obviously ill at ease at her unexpected appearance.

Judy hated to fluster him. "I have some letters I'd like to mail."

"Of course."

Judy raised questioning eyes to his. "They're to my family?" She made the statement a question, asking if there'd be any objection. "Do you have regular mail delivery to and from the island?"

"All correspondence is handled by courier."

"Then there's no problem with writing my father?"

"None whatsoever."

Judy hated to be suspicious, but Avery didn't sound all that confident, and it would be easy for him to deceive her.

"I'll see to it personally if that will reassure you, Ms. Lovin." McFarland's voice behind her was brisk and businesslike.

Judy blushed painfully as she faced him. "I'd appreciate th-that," she said, stammering slightly. The virility of his smile made her catch her breath. That morning, when they were out riding, he'd been sneering at her and now she could feel her pulse react to a simple lift of his mouth.

"Thank you, John," she said softly.

"John?" Avery Anderson echoed, perplexed, but his voice sounded as though it had come from another room—another world.

"Would you care to see my office?" McFarland asked, but the sparkle in his eyes made Judy wonder if he was taunting her.

"I don't want to interrupt your day." Already she was retreating from him, taking small, even steps as she backed away from Avery Anderson's desk. "Perhaps another time."

"As you wish." His eyes grew perceptibly gentler at her bemused look. "We'll talk tonight, during dinner."

The words were as much a command as an invitation. It was understood that she'd show up in the dining room when called.

Judy nodded. "At dinner."

By the time she closed the doors to her suite, her heart was thumping wildly. She attempted to tell herself she feared John McFarland, but that wasn't entirely true—the man was an enigma. But instead of gauging her responses by his mood, Judy decided she could only be herself.

She dressed for dinner in a black skirt and a blouse that had been favorites of her father's. Charles had said the pink and maroon stripes enhanced the brown of her eyes, reminding him of her mother.

At the top of the stairs, Judy placed her hand on the railing, then paused. She was excited about this dinner, yet apprehensive. Her stomach rebelled at the thought of food, but she yearned to know this man—"the Beast." Exactly why he'd brought her to St. Steven's had yet to be explained. She had a right to know; she *needed* to know. Surely that wasn't too much to ask.

He was standing by the fireplace, sipping wine, when she entered the dining room. Once again she was struck by his virility. He, too, had dressed formally, in a pinstriped suit that revealed broad, muscular shoulders and narrow hips.

"Good evening, Judy."

She smiled and noted that he'd used her given name for the first time. Some of the tension drained out of her.

"John."

"Would you care for a glass of wine before dinner?"

"Please." The inside of her mouth felt as though it was stuffed with cotton. The wine would help...or it might drown whatever wit she still possessed. As he approached her with a goblet, Judy was unsure whether she should take it. His blue eyes burned into her, and, without further thought, Judy accepted the wine.

"Why do you hate my father?" she asked, the words slipping from her mouth as she met his gaze.

"On the contrary, I hold him in high regard."

Judy's eyes widened with disbelief.

"Charles Lovin has more grit than twenty men half his age."

"You mean because he's managed to hold you off against impossible odds?"

"Not so impossible," McFarland

countered, before taking a sip of wine. "I did allow him a means of escape."

Judy considered his statement, momentarily baffled by his reasoning. "You wanted me on the island," she said.

"Yes, you."

It wasn't as though he desired her company. In the two days since her arrival, he'd barely spoken to her; indeed, he seemed to avoid doing so.

"But why? What possible good am I to you?"

"None at all. I require no one." A hardness descended over his features, and his eyes narrowed, his expression shutting her out. His face showed his arrogance—and his pride. Judy frowned, aching to soothe the hurt, erase it from his life. She longed to understand what made him the way he was. Somehow, somewhere, a cruel and heartless person had mortally wounded

John McFarland's spirit. From the torment in his eyes, she knew the scars hadn't healed.

"Am I to be your slave?" she asked, without anger, her voice even.

"No."

"Y-your pet?"

"Don't be ridiculous!" he shouted. "You're free to do as you wish."

"Can I leave?"

He gave a curt laugh and took another sip of his wine. "You're here to amuse me."

"For how long?"

He shrugged. "Until you cease doing so."

Muted footsteps drew Judy's attention to the manservant who stood just inside the dining room. He nodded once in McFarland's direction.

"I believe our dinner is ready. Chicken Béarnaise." He moved to her end of the table and held out her chair.

Judy was grateful for the opportunity to sit down; her legs felt wobbly. No man had ever affected her the way John did. But he claimed he needed no one, and by all outward appearances he was right.

Once she was seated, John took the chair at the opposite end of the table.

Judy spread out the linen napkin on her lap. "I came across some children today," she said after several tense minutes.

"There are a number of families who live on the island."

"The kids were friendly. At first I wasn't sure they spoke English, but then I realized that they speak it so fast it sounds like a foreign language."

John smiled at that. "I haven't had the opportunity to talk to them myself, but I'll remember that when I do."

"They asked about you."

"The children?"

"Yes, they call you the Dark Prince."

A brief smile flickered across his face. "They usually avoid me."

"I know."

Humor flashed in his eyes as he studied her. Once again, she'd surprised him. He'd expected her to be outraged, spitting angry tirades at him, ruining his meal. Instead, she sat at his table with the subtle grace of royalty when he knew she must be dying inside at his callousness.

"If they call me the Dark Prince, did they give *you* a name?"

Judy shifted her gaze. "I asked them to call me Judy."

"But they didn't."

"No." Color invaded her face, and she obviously had difficulty swallowing.

"Tell me what they decided to call you."

"I—I'd prefer not to."

"Finding out would be a simple matter," he said in low, unthreatening tones.

Judy found little amusement in her predicament. "They called me 'the Dark Prince's woman.' I tried to explain that I was only a friend, but it didn't seem to do any good. This probably embarrasses you, but I couldn't seem to change their minds."

McFarland felt the laughter leave his face. He'd meant to tease her, but she was concerned that these people, these strangers who occupied his land, had offended him by suggesting she was his woman. He felt as though someone had given him a swift kick in the behind. He raised his eyes, studying her to be sure she wasn't taunting him, and knew in his heart that it wasn't in her to insult man or beast. And he was both.

Their meal arrived, but McFarland

had little appetite. "Do you like the island?" he asked, wanting to hear her speak again. The sound of her voice was soothing to him.

"It's lovely."

"If there's anything you wish, you need only ask."

"There's nothing." Judy saw that his tone, his look, everything about him, had changed. His mocking arrogance had vanished; no longer did he look as though he meant to admonish her for some imagined wrong, or punish her for being her father's daughter. She found it impossible to eat.

"Do you dislike the solitude?"

She searched his face, wondering why he cared. "It's not Manhattan, but that's fine. To be honest, I needed a vacation and this is as close to paradise as I'm likely to find."

"You've had a nap."

She nodded.

"You're to have complete run of the house and island."

"Thank you, John," she said humbly, "you've been very kind."

Kind? He'd been kind to force her into staying here? Kind to have blackmailed her into leaving everything familiar in her life? He stared at her, not understanding how she could even suggest such a thing. Abruptly, he pushed aside his plate and stood. "If you'll excuse me, I have some business matters that require my attention."

"Of course."

He stormed out of the room as if she'd offended him. For a full minute, Judy sat frozen, uncertain of what had happened between them. He had seemed to want her company, then despised it.

She, too, had no desire to finish her meal, and feeling at odds with herself, she stood. It was still early, and she had no intention of returning to her rooms. John had said she could freely explore the house and she'd barely seen half of it.

Judy never made it beyond the center hall. The doors were what had attracted her most. The huge mahogany panels stretched from the ceiling to the polished floor, reminding her of ancient castles. Unable to resist, she turned both handles, pushed open the massive doors and entered the dimly lit room.

She paused just inside, and sighed with pure pleasure. It was a library, elegantly decorated with comfortable leather chairs, two desks and a variety of tables and lamps. Every wall was filled with books. Judy couldn't have been more pleased if she'd inadvertently stumbled upon a treasure. A flip of the switch bathed the room in light and she hurried forward to investigate.

An hour later, when the clock chimed, Judy was astonished to realize how long she'd been there. Reverently, she folded back the pages of a first edition of Charles Dickens's *A Christmas Carol*. Each book she saw produced a feeling of awe and respect. Mingled with the classics were volumes of modern literature; one entire wall was dedicated to nonfiction.

With such a wide variety to choose from, Judy finally selected a science fiction novel. She sat in a high-backed leather chair and read for an hour before slipping off her shoes and tucking her feet beneath her. Suddenly thirsty, she went to the meticulous kitchen and made herself a cup of tea. Carrying it into the library, Judy returned to her chair.

McFarland found her there after midnight, sleeping contentedly in the chair, her legs curled under her. Her head was nestled against the upholstery, with one arm carelessly draped over her face. The other dangled limply at her side so that the tips of her fingers almost touched the Persian carpet. Transfixed, he stood there for a moment studying her, unable to look away.

A tender feeling weakened him, and he sat in the chair opposite hers. For a long time, he was content to do nothing but watch her sleep. He wondered at the wealth of emotion she aroused in him. He knew it wasn't love—not even close. He felt protective toward her and yearned to take away the troubles that plagued this young woman's life. Surprisingly, he wanted her to be happy.

She looked as innocent as a child, but was very much a woman. She was gentle and kind, honorable without being lofty. Generous without being a pushover. He'd never known a woman like her, and was shocked to find himself consumed with fear. He could hurt Judy Lovin, hurt her beyond anything she'd known in her life, hurt her more than Richard, who'd stolen her trust and wounded her heart with his greed.

McFarland knew she'd fall in love with him at the slightest encouragement. His conjecture wasn't based on ego, but on the knowledge that Judy, by nature, was giving and loving. If he were to ask, she would deny him nothing. His own power frightened him, but that wasn't what stopped him. He wasn't any knight in shining armor. No, the simple truth was that the thought of Judy's control over him was more terrifying than any pleasure he'd get from obtaining her love.

He considered waking her and it seemed only natural to lean over and kiss her. Her lips would be soft under his. He pictured her raising her arms and hugging his neck. She would smile at him and they'd stare at each other. She'd blush in that way she had that made her all the more beautiful, and she'd lower her thick lashes as she struggled to hide her feelings from him.

Forcefully, McFarland's fingers clenched the arm of the leather chair. He'd have a maid wake Judy and see her to her room.

She was just a woman, he reminded himself, and no doubt there were a million others like her. Who needed Judy Lovin? Not him.

"Midnight," Judy called, standing on the bottom rung of the corral fence. "If you want it, you'll have to come to me." She held out the carrot to the prancing black horse, who snorted and pawed the ground.

"It's yours for the taking," she said

soothingly. Winning the trust of the
sleek, black horse had become para-
mount in the four days that had passed
since the night she'd fallen asleep in
the library. John had been avoiding
her; Judy was convinced of that. The
only times they were together were at
dinner, and he was always preoccupied
with business, avoiding conversation
and generally ignoring her.

Judy wasn't offended as much as
bewildered. At any moment, she half
expected to receive word that he no
longer required her presence on St. Steven's, or some other stiffly worded de-
cree. She'd be happy to leave, although
she'd miss the children, who had fast
become her friends. She'd been on the
island a week now and surely that was
enough time to serve whatever purpose
he had in mind.

But she *would* miss the children. She
met them daily now on the beach. They

brought her small, homemade gifts—a flowerpot and a hat both woven from palm leaves, cleverly done. A huge conch shell and a hundred smaller ones had been given to her with great ceremony. In return she told them stories, laughed at their antics and played their games. She met their mothers and visited their homes. She would miss them, but she wouldn't forget them.

"Midnight," she coaxed again. "I know you want this carrot." If John wouldn't allow her to be his friend, then she'd work on the horse. Judy had noticed several similarities between the two; both were angry, arrogant, proud.

The horse remained in the farthest corner of the corral, as determined to ignore her as John seemed to be.

"I suppose all the women tell you how good-looking you are?" she said with a laugh. "But I'm not going to say that. You're much too conceited already."

Midnight bowed his powerful head and snorted.

"I thought that would get you." Jumping down from the fence, Judy approached the gate. "You're really going to make me come to you, aren't you?"

The stallion pranced around the yard, his tail arched.

"You devil," Judy said with a loud sigh. "All this time together and you're more stubborn now than when I started."

The horse continued to ignore her.

"What if I told you I had a handful of sugar cubes in my pocket?" She patted her hip. "Sweet, sweet sugar cubes that will melt in your mouth." As she spoke, she released the clasp to the gate and let herself into the corral.

Midnight paused and stared at her, throwing his head back and forth. "You'll have to come closer, though," she said softly.

His hoof dug at the hard dirt.

"Honestly, horse, you're more stubborn than your master."

She took three steps toward the huge black stallion, who paused to study her. He jerked his neck, tossing his thick mane.

With one hand on her hip, Judy shook her head. "You don't fool me one bit."

Someone walked up behind her, but Judy paid no attention, suspecting it was Sam. He was bound to be angry with her. He'd told her repeatedly not to go inside the corral, but since Midnight refused to come to her, she'd decided she had no choice.

"Don't move." John's steel-edged words cut through her. "If you value your life, don't move."

Four

Judy went still, her heart pounding wildly. She wanted to turn and assure John that Midnight wouldn't hurt her. She longed to tell him she'd been working for days, gaining the stallion's trust. All her life she'd had a way with animals and children. Her father claimed she could make a wounded bear her friend. Midnight had a fiery nature; it was what made him such a magnificent horse. He'd been a challenge, but she believed he'd never purposely injure her. But Judy said none of these things. She couldn't. John's voice had been so cold, so cutting, that she dared not defy him.

The clicking sound behind her told Judy that Midnight's master had entered the corral. He walked past her and his clipped, even stride revealed his fierce anger. He didn't even glance at her and as she noticed the hard look in his eyes, she was glad.

Midnight pranced around the corral, his satiny black head held high, his tail arched, his hooves kicking up loose dirt.

McFarland gave one shrill whistle, to which the stallion responded without delay. Midnight cocked his head and galloped past Judy to his master's side, coming to an abrupt halt. He lowered his head. With one smooth movement, McFarland gripped the horse's mane and swung onto his back. Midnight protested violently and reared, kicking his powerful front legs.

Judy sucked in her breath, afraid that McFarland wouldn't have time to gain control of the animal. She was wrong; when the horse planted his feet on the ground, John was in charge.

"Get out."

The words were sharp and he didn't so much as look at her, but then he didn't need to. She could feel his contempt and his anger. Judy did as he said.

McFarland circled the paddock a few times before swinging off the stallion's back and joining her at the corral gate.

"You stupid idiot," he hissed. He grabbed her by the shoulders and gave her one vicious jerk. "You could've been killed!"

When he released her, Judy stumbled backward. Her eyes were wide with fear. In all her life no one had ever spo-

ken to her in such a menacing tone.
No one had dared raise a hand to her.
Now she faced the wounded bear, and
was forced to admit that Charles Lovin
had been right—John McFarland was
a beast no woman could tame.

"Who let you inside the corral?"

Her throat had thickened, making
speech impossible. Even if she'd been
able to answer him, she wouldn't have.
Sam had no idea she'd ever been near
Midnight.

"Sam!" McFarland barked the stableman's name.

The older man rushed out of the
barn, limping. His face was red and a
sheen of perspiration had broken out
on his forehead.

McFarland attacked him with a bar-
rage of swear words. He ended by or-
dering the man to pack his bags.

Sam went pale.

"No," Judy cried.

McFarland turned on her, his eyes as cutting as his words. He stood no more than a foot from her, bearing down on her as he shouted, using language that made her gasp. Her eyes widened as she searched his face, attempting to hide her fear. Her chin trembled with the effort to maintain her composure as she squarely met his cold gaze, unwilling to let him know how much he intimidated her.

McFarland couldn't make himself stop shouting at her. The boiling anger erupted like fire from a volcano. By chance, he'd happened to look out his window and he'd seen Judy as she opened the corral gate. The fear had nearly paralyzed him. All he could think of was getting to her, warning her. A picture of Midnight's powerful legs striking out at her had almost driven him insane. He hadn't been angry then, but now he burned with it.

McFarland could see the shock running through Judy's veins as the pulse at the base of her throat pounded frantically. Still, the words came and he hated himself for subjecting her to his uncontrollable tantrum.

"Anyone who pulls an asinine trick like this doesn't deserve to be around good horses," he shouted. "You're a hazard to everyone here. I don't want you near my stables again. Is that understood?"

Her head jerked back as though he'd slapped her.

"Yes." She nodded weakly, signaling that she'd abide by his edict.

She left him then, with such dignity that it took all his strength not to run after her and beg her forgiveness.

The air was electrified and McFarland rammed his hand through his hair.

Sam stood there, accusing him, silently reprimanding him with every breath. The older man had once been a friend; now his censure scorched McFarland.

"I'll be out of here by morning," Sam muttered, and with a look of disgust, he turned away.

The remainder of the day was a waste. McFarland couldn't stop thinking of what he'd said to Judy, and he experienced more than a twinge of conscience. That woman had eyes that could tear apart a man's soul. When he'd ordered her to stay away from the horses, she'd returned his look with confused pain, as though that was the last thing she'd expected. He had wanted to pull her into his arms, hold her against his chest and feel the assurance of her heart beating close to his. Instead, he'd lashed out at her, unmercifully striking at her pride when all he'd really wanted to do was protect her.

His vehement feelings shocked him most. He tried to tell himself that Judy deserved every word he'd said. She must have been crazy to get into a pen with an animal as unpredictable as Midnight. He'd warned her about him; so had Sam. Anyone with a brain would have known better. There were times when even he couldn't handle that stallion.

Damn! McFarland slammed his fist against the desk. He couldn't afford to feel like this toward a woman. Any woman, but particularly Judy Lovin.

As she came down the stairs for dinner that evening, Judy's stomach tightened and fluttered with nerves. Her face continued to burn with humiliation. She would've preferred to have dinner sent to her room and completely avoid John, but she had to face the beast for Sam's sake.

"Good evening, John," she said quietly as she entered the dining room.

He stood with his back to her, staring out the window. He turned abruptly, unable to disguise his surprise. From all appearances, he hadn't expected to see her.

"Judy."

They stood staring at each other before taking their places at the elegant table.

Not a word was exchanged during the entire meal. In all her memory, Judy couldn't recall a more awkward dinner. Neither had much appetite; eating was a pretense. Only after their plates had been removed and their coffee poured did she dare appeal to the man across the table from her.

"Although I'd rather not talk about

what happened this afternoon, I feel we need to discuss Sam."

John took a sip of his coffee. His eyes narrowed slightly, and he seemed affronted that she'd approach him on a matter he was sure to consider none of her business.

She clutched her napkin and forced herself to continue. "If you make Sam leave the island you might as well cut off both his legs. St. Steven's is his home. The horses are his family. What happened wasn't his fault. He'd told me repeatedly to stay away from Midnight. If he'd known I'd gone into that corral he would've had my hide. I snuck in there when Sam wasn't looking. He doesn't deserve to lose his job because of me."

John lowered his cup to the saucer without speaking.

"Despite everything people say

about you, John McFarland, I trust you to be fair."

He arched his brows at that comment. This woman had played havoc with his afternoon, caused him to alienate a man he'd considered a friend, and now she seemed to believe that by pleading softly she could wrap him around her little finger.

"Sam leaves in the morning, as scheduled."

Without ceremony, she rose from her chair. Her eyes steadily held his. "I see now that I misread you," she told him. "My judgment is usually better, but that isn't important now." She turned to leave the room. After only a few steps, she paused and looked back. "My father once told me something, but I didn't fully appreciate his wisdom until this moment. He's right. No man is so weak as one who cannot admit he's wrong."

By the time she reached her rooms, Judy discovered she was shaking. She sat on the edge of her bed and closed her eyes. The disillusionment was almost more than she could bear. She'd been mistaken about John McFarland. He was a wild, untamable beast—the most dangerous kind...one without a heart.

Several hours passed, and although John had forbidden her to go near the stables again, Judy couldn't stay away. She had to talk to Sam, tell him how deeply sorry she was.

She changed from her dress into shorts and a T-shirt. As usual the house was silent as she slipped down the stairs and out the front door.

Even the night seemed sullen and disenchanted. The still, heavy air was oppressive. The area around the house was well lit, but the stable was far enough away to be enveloped in heavy shadows. The moon shone dimly and provided little light.

As Judy walked along the path that led to the stables, she felt a chill invade her limbs. She longed for home and the comfort of familiarity. Folding her arms around her middle, she sighed. She tried not to wonder how long John intended to keep her on the island. Surely he'd send her away soon. After the incident with Midnight, he must be eager to get rid of her. She was a thorn in his side—a festering one.

Not for the first time did she feel like an unwelcome stranger to the island. Although she'd done everything possible to make the best of the situation, she was still John's prisoner. In the days since her arrival, she'd struggled to create some normalcy in her life. She'd begun to feel at ease. Now that had changed. Without access to Princess, she wouldn't be able to see the children as frequently and with Sam's dismissal, the other servants would avoid her, fearing they, too, could lose their positions. Loneliness would overwhelm her.

The door to the stable was open, revealing the silhouette of Sam's elongated shadow. His actions were quick and sure and Judy strained her ears, thinking she heard the soft trill of his whistle.

"Evening, Sam," she said, pausing just inside the open doorway.

"Ms. Lovin." His eyes brightened with delight, then quickly faded as he glanced around. "Ms. Lovin, you shouldn't be here—"

"I know," she said gently, interrupting him. "I came to tell you how sorry I am."

He shrugged his shoulders, seemingly unconcerned. "Don't you worry about that. It's all taken care of now."

The words took a moment to sink in. "You mean you aren't leaving?"

Sam rubbed the side of his jaw and cocked his head. "I've never known Mr. McFarland to change his mind. A man doesn't become as wealthy as that one without being decisive. I knew I'd done wrong to let you get close to that stallion—I figured I deserved what I got. Can't say I agree with the way he laid into you, though, you being a lady and all, but you took it well."

"You aren't leaving the island?" Judy repeated, still not convinced she could believe what she was hearing.

"No. Mr. McFarland came to me, said he'd overreacted. He asked me personally to stay on. I don't mind telling you I was surprised."

So was Judy. She felt warm and wonderful. The sensation was so strong that she closed her eyes for a moment. She hadn't misjudged John. He was everything she hoped.

"Mr. McFarland's here now," Sam continued, his voice low. "Midnight's still in the corral and he went out there. I don't suppose you saw him or you wouldn't be here." The man who ruled the stables removed his hat and wiped his forehead, then gave Judy a sheepish grin. "He didn't say anything to me about letting you in the stables again."

"I'll leave," she said, unable to restrain a smile. Sam was back in John's good graces, and she'd become a threat.

The older man paused and looked around before whispering, "You come see me anytime you want. Princess will miss you if you don't bring her a carrot every now and then."

Judy laughed and gently placed her hand on his forearm. "Thank you, Sam."

He grinned in response, and she was grateful that she could count him as her friend.

Judy left the barn, intent on escaping before John discovered her presence. Her world had righted itself and there was no reason to topple it again—at least not this soon.

She was halfway to the house when she changed her mind, realizing she wanted to thank John. Like his stallion, he was dangerous and unpredictable. He was different from any man she'd ever known, and it frightened her how much she wanted to be with him. How much she wanted to thank him for not firing Sam.

John's shadow moved in and out of the dim moonlight as she approached. As Sam had told her, he stood by the corral, one booted foot braced against the bottom rung, his arms resting on the top.

A minute or so later she joined him. "It's a lovely night, isn't it?" she said, tentatively leaning against the fence.

McFarland tensed, his face hard and unyielding. He avoided looking at her. "There's a storm brewing."

"No," she said with a soft smile. "The storm has passed."

He gave a low, self-mocking laugh. "I asked you to stay away from here."

"I won't come again if you wish."

What he wished would have shocked her all the way to those dainty feet of hers, just as it had shocked him. He liked his women spicy and hot; Judy Lovin was sweet and warm.

"I'd like to show you something," she said, breaking into his thoughts. "But I need your trust."

He didn't answer her one way or the other. All evening he'd been toying with the idea of sending her back to her family and he was at a loss to understand why that no longer appealed to him. The woman had become a nuisance. She forced him to look deep within himself; she invaded his dreams and haunted his days. He hadn't had a moment's peace since she'd stepped onto the island.

"John, will you trust me for one moment?"

He turned his head slightly.

Standing on the bottom rung of the corral, she gave a shrill whistle that was an imitation of the one John had used earlier that day to attract Midnight's attention.

The stallion snorted once, jerked his head and casually walked toward her.

"Here, boy," she said, patting his nose and rubbing her hands and face over his as he nuzzled her. "No, I don't have any sugar cubes with me now, but I will another day. I wanted to show your master that we're friends."

Midnight whinnied softly and seemed to object when she stepped down and moved away.

McFarland wouldn't have been any more shocked if she'd pulled out a gun and fired on him. She'd made Midnight look as tame as a child's pony. His throat tightened.

"I was never in any real danger," she explained in a low voice. "Midnight and I are friends. Most of his arrogance is show. It's expected of him and he likes to live up to his reputation."

"When?" McFarland growled.

"I've been working with him in the afternoons. We made our peace two days ago. He'd even let me ride him if I wanted to, but he's your horse and I wouldn't infringe on that."

Why not? She had infringed on everything else in his life! His peace of mind had been shot from the minute she'd turned those incredible eyes on him.

Without a word, he left her standing at the corral, not trusting himself to speak.

Hours later, unable to sleep, McFarland gazed around his still bedroom. He didn't know what to make of Judy Lovin; she could be either angel or demon. She tamed wild animals, was beloved by children and made his cynical heart pound with desires that were only a little short of pure lust.

The maid woke Judy early the next morning just as dawn dappled the countryside.

"Mr. McFarland is waiting for you, miss."

Judy sat up in bed and rubbed the sleep from her eyes. "Mr. McFarland?"

"He's at the stables, miss."

"He wants me to go riding with him?"

"I believe so."

With a surge of energy, Judy tossed back the covers and climbed out of bed. "Could you please tell him I'll be there in ten minutes?"

"Right away."

Judy was breathless by the time she arrived at the stables. Princess was saddled and waiting for her; Midnight stood beside the mare. John appeared from inside the barn.

"Good morning," she said brightly. He was dressed in black again, his eyes a deep indigo-blue. "It's a glorious morning, isn't it?"

"Glorious," he echoed mockingly.

She decided to ignore his derision. The earth smelled fresh in the aftermath of the night's storm. The dewdrops beaded like sparkling emeralds on the lush green foliage.

"Are you ready?" McFarland asked as he mounted.

"Yes." She swung onto Princess's back.

As he had the first time she'd ridden with him, John rode furiously. Judy was able to keep pace with him, but when they reached the far side of the island, she was exhausted from the workout.

He slowed, and they trotted side by side on the flawless beach.

"You never cease to amaze me," he said, studying her. He'd ridden hard and long, half expecting her to fall behind, almost wishing she had.

"Me? I find *you* astonishing. Do you always ride like that?"

"No," he admitted sheepishly.

"You must've been born in the saddle."

"Hardly. I'd made my first million before I ever owned a horse."

"When was that?"

A slow, sensual smile formed as he glanced in her direction. "You're full of questions, aren't you?"

"Does it bother you?"

He stared at her. "No, I suppose not."

"I imagine you had a colorful youth."

He laughed outright at that. "I'd been arrested twice before I was thirteen."

"Arrested?" Her eyes widened. "But why?"

"I was a thief." He threw back his head and laughed. "Some say I still am."

Judy dismissed his joking. "I don't believe that. You're an honorable man. You wouldn't take anything that didn't belong to you, not without a good reason."

Her automatic defense of him produced a curious hurt in his chest. There *had* been a good reason—someone had tried to cheat him. In the same circumstances, he'd react the same way. He wasn't bad, but in all his life, only one man had ever believed in him. From grade school, he'd been branded a renegade, a hellion. He'd been all that and more. But he wouldn't be where he was today if he hadn't been willing to gamble. He'd had to be tough.

When he didn't respond, Judy sought his gaze. The look in his eyes made her ache inside. He wore the wounds of his past proudly, like medals of valor, but the scars went deep.

"What about you?" he taunted. "Haven't you ever done anything wrong? Other than falling in love with a married man?"

The pain in her eyes was so clear that McFarland felt ashamed of asking.

"Actually, I have," she said, recovering quickly. "But since you don't know, I'm not going to tell you."

She laughed, slapped the reins against Princess's neck and sped off, leaving a cloud of sand in her wake.

McFarland caught up with her easily.

She smiled at him, her brown eyes sparkling. Dismounting, she brushed the wind-tossed hair from her face and stared into the sun. "I love this island. I love the seclusion and the peace. No wonder you had to have it."

McFarland joined her on the beach. He knew he was going to kiss her, knew he'd regret it later, but he was beyond caring. He touched her shoulder and turned her so that she faced him, giving her ample opportunity to stop him if she wanted to.

She didn't. Her pulse surged as his mouth moved to cover hers.

His arms went around her, bringing her close. He groaned and dragged his mouth away. She tasted like paradise and he didn't know how he could avoid wanting more. "I wish I hadn't done that," he said with a moan.

"I'm glad you did," she whispered.

"Don't tell me that."

"Yes…"

She wasn't allowed to finish as he held her face and kissed her again, unable to get enough of her. She leaned against him, letting him absorb her weight. Their bodies were pressed close. His fingers became tangled in her hair as he kissed her. He felt a tremor work its way through her and heard the soft sounds of passion that slid from her throat.

Instantly, he sobered, breaking off the kiss.

Judy sagged against him and released a long breath, resting her forehead on his chest. "You kiss the same way you ride."

McFarland slowly rubbed his chin against her hair as a lazy smile touched his mouth. She made him tremble from the inside out. He'd been right the first time; he shouldn't have let this happen. He should've found the strength to resist. Now that he'd held her, now that he'd kissed her, there was no turning back.

"John?"

He wanted to blame her for what she did to him, punish her for dominating his thoughts and making him hunger for her touch, but he didn't. He couldn't. His rage was directed solely at himself.

"I shouldn't have said those things."

"I know," she whispered. She seemed to sense intuitively that he was talking about Midnight. "I understand."

"Why didn't you say something?"

"I couldn't—you were too angry. I'd frightened you."

He slipped his arm around her shoulder. He should be begging forgiveness, but all she seemed to do was offer excuses for him. "I want to make it up to you," he said.

"There's no need. It's forgotten."

"No," he said forcefully. "I won't pass it off as lightly as that. Anything you want is yours. Just name it."

She went still.

"Except leaving the island." There must be a thousand things she longed to own, he thought. Jewels, land, maybe stocks and bonds. He'd give them to her. He'd give her anything she asked for.

"John, please, there's no need. I—"

"Name it." His eyes hardened.

She bit her lower lip, realizing it would do little good to argue. He was making amends the only way he knew how—with money. "Anything?"

He nodded sharply.

"Then I want the school on the island rebuilt. It's run-down and badly in need of repairs and unsafe for the children."

Five

Paulo, a gleeful year-old baby, rested on Judy's hip. Other children followed her around the cluster of homes as though she were royalty. The small party walked to the outskirts of the schoolyard, where the workers were busily constructing the new schoolhouse.

"Mr. McFarland told me the school will be ready by the end of the month," Judy told the children. The building had gone up so quickly that it had as-

tonished both Judy and the islanders.
The day after she'd made her request,
a construction crew had arrived, followed by several shiploads of building
supplies. Judy shuddered to think of
the expense, but John hadn't so much
as blinked when she said she wanted a
school. And when John McFarland ordered something, there were no delays.

Paulo's mother joined Judy and the
other children. The baby gurgled excitedly, stretched out his arms and leaned
toward his mother. Judy gave him a
kiss and handed him over.

"Paulo likes you."

"As long as his mother isn't around,"
Judy responded with a laugh.

"The children are very happy," the
shy young woman added, looking toward the school. "Thank you."

"Don't thank me. Mr. McFarland's
having it built, not me."

"But you're his woman and you're the one who told him…."

Judy had long since given up explaining that she wasn't John's "woman," although the thought wasn't as objectionable as when she'd first come here. In the weeks since, her attitude toward John had altered dramatically. He was the beast her father claimed; Judy had seen that side of him on more than one occasion. But he possessed a gentleness, too, a kindness that touched her heart.

Now that she knew him better, she hoped to understand his idiosyncrasies. He'd told her so little of his life, but from what she'd gleaned, he'd been abandoned at a young age and raised in a series of foster homes. A high-school teacher had befriended him, encouraged his talents and helped him start his first business. Although the teacher had died before John had achieved his financial empire, the island had been named after him—Steven Fischer.

Since the kiss they'd shared that early morning, Judy's relationship with John had changed subtly. As before, he didn't seek out her company and the only time she could count on being with him was at dinner. She was allowed to take Princess whenever she wished, but the invitation to ride with John had come only twice. He treated her with the politeness due to a houseguest, but avoided any physical contact, which told her that he regretted having kissed her.

Judy didn't regret it. She thought about that morning often, relived it again and again, fantasizing, wishing it hadn't ended so quickly.

She exchanged letters with her family regularly now. Her father and her brother worried about her, but Judy frequently assured them she was happy, and to her surprise, realized it was the truth. She missed her old life, her family and her home, but she kept them close in her heart and didn't dwell on the separation.

John had given no indication when she could return and she hadn't asked. For now she was content.

After spending the morning with the children, Judy went back to the house, wearing a wreath of flowers on her head. The children and Paulo's mother had woven it for her and she'd been touched by their generosity.

Since it was an hour until lunch, Judy decided to find a new book to read. The library doors were open and beckoned her inside. Judy walked into the room.

McFarland sat at the desk, writing.

"John," she said, surprised. "I'm sorry, I didn't mean to intrude."

He glanced up and the frown that

creased his forehead relaxed at the sight of her. She wore a simple yellow sundress with a halo of flowers on her thick, dark hair. He couldn't pull his eyes away from her.

"You didn't disturb me," he told her.

"It's a fantastic morning," she said eagerly, seeking a topic of conversation.

In the weeks since her arrival, Judy had acquired a rich, golden tan. Her healthy glow mesmerized him. "Beauty" did little to describe this woman, whose charm and winsome elegance appealed to him so strongly. McFarland had never known anyone like her. Her goodness wasn't a sweet coating that disguised a greedy heart. Judy Lovin was pure and good; her simple presence humbled him.

The memory of their kiss played havoc with his senses. He hadn't touched her since, doing his utmost to be the congenial host. The sweetest torment he'd ever endured was having her so close and not making love to her. He feared what would happen if he kissed her again, and yet the dream of doing so constantly interrupted his sleep.

He'd planned to return Judy to her family before now, but couldn't bring himself to do so. He was at odds with himself, knowing it was foolish to keep her on the island with him. If she'd revealed some sign of being unhappy and asked to go home to New York, he would've allowed it, but Judy showed no desire to leave and he selfishly wanted to keep her with him, despite her family's constant pleading.

"I spent the morning with the children," Judy said, still only a few steps inside the room. "They're excited about the school."

John nodded, unconcerned. "Did they give you the flowers?"

She raised one hand to her head, having forgotten about the orchid wreath. "Yes, they're talented, aren't they?" Out of the corner of her eye, she saw an elaborate chess set. When he didn't respond to her first question, she asked another. "Do you play?"

McFarland's gaze followed her own. "On occasion."

"Are you busy now?"

He glanced at his watch, more for show than anything. He was always busy, but not too busy to torture himself with her. "Not terribly."

"Shall we play a game, then?" She longed for his company. "That is, if it wouldn't be an intrusion."

His eyes held hers; he couldn't refuse her. "All right," he agreed.

"Good," she said, smiling, and

brought the chess set to the desk, then pulled up a chair to sit opposite him.

"Shall we make it interesting?" McFarland asked, leaning forward.

"Money?"

He grinned. "No."

"What then?"

"Let the winner decide."

"But…"

"How good are you?"

Judy dropped her gaze to the board. "Fair. If I lose, what would you want from me?"

What a question. The possibilities sent his blood pressure soaring. He wanted her heart and her soul. And he wanted to feel her body beneath his own. The image clawed at his mind and his senses. He forced himself to rein in his desire.

"John?"

"What would I want?" he repeated hurriedly. "I don't know. Something simple. What about you? What would you want?"

Her laughter echoed off the book-lined walls. "Something simple," she echoed.

His eyes softened as he studied her. Afraid that he'd be caught staring, McFarland tried to look away and discovered that he couldn't—her eyes held his.

"It's your move."

McFarland brought his attention to the board, unaware that she'd placed her pawn in play. "Right." He responded automatically, sliding his own man forward.

By sheer force of will, he was able to concentrate on the game. Her technique was straightforward and uncomplicated and a few moves later, he determined that her strategy was weak. He should be able to put her in checkmate within ten or fifteen minutes, but he wasn't sure he wanted to. If he lost, albeit deliberately, he'd be obligated to give her "something simple." He thought about how she'd look in a diamond necklace and doubted that the jewels could compete with her smile. Emeralds would draw out the rich color of her deep brown eyes, but no necklace could do her eyes justice. A sapphire brooch perhaps. Or...

"John? It's your turn."

Slightly embarrassed to be caught dreaming, he slipped his bishop forward with the intent of capturing her knight, which was in a vulnerable position.

Judy hesitated. "That wasn't a good move, John. Would you like to do it over?"

He agreed with her; it wasn't a brilliant play, but adequate. "No, I released my hand from the bishop."

"You're sure?"

He studied the pieces again. He didn't think he was in imminent danger of losing his king or the match. If he did forfeit the game it would be on his terms. "Even if this was a bad move, which it isn't," he added hastily, "I wouldn't change it."

Her eyes fairly danced with excitement. "So be it, then." She lifted her rook, raised her eyes to his before setting it beside his undefended king, and announced, "Checkmate."

Tight-lipped, John analyzed her play and was astonished to discover she was right. So much for her being straightforward and uncomplicated! The woman had duped him with as much skill as a double agent. The first couple of plays had been executed to give him a sense of false security while she set him up for the kill.

"I won," she reminded him. "And according to our agreement, I'm entitled to something simple."

McFarland still hadn't taken his eyes off the chessboard. The little schemer. Now that he could see how she'd done it, he was impressed with her cunning and skill. All right. He'd lost in a fair game; he was ready for her to name her price.

"Okay," he said a bit stiffly. "What would you like? A diamond necklace?"

She looked horrified. "Oh, no! Nothing like that."

"What then? A car?"

For an instant she was too stunned to reply. "Good heavens, no. Your idea of something simple and mine seem to be entirely different."

"What do you want then?"

"Your time."

His expression grew puzzled. "My what?"

"Time," she repeated. "You work

much too hard. I don't recall even one afternoon when you weren't cooped up in that stuffy office. You own a small piece of paradise. You should enjoy it more often."

"So what's that got to do with anything?"

"For my prize I want us to pack a lunch and take it to the beach. It'll be a relaxing afternoon for both of us."

He grinned at the idea that she would assume he had a few hours to do nothing but laze on the beach. Surely she wasn't so naive that she didn't know he ruled a financial empire. Offices around the globe were awaiting his decisions. "I don't have time for that nonsense," he finally said.

"That's a shame." Judy looped a dark strand of hair around her ear. "Unfortunately, you're the one who decided to place a wager on our chess match. You should never have made the suggestion if you weren't willing to follow through."

"I'll buy you something instead. I know just the thing."

Judy shook her head adamantly. "I would've sworn you were a man who kept his promises. The only thing I want is this afternoon."

He frowned. "I can't afford to waste time lollygagging around the beach."

"Yes, John."

"There are cost sheets, reports, financial statements—all of which need to be reviewed."

"Yes, John."

"There are decisions to be made." His voice rose in volume. "Offers to be considered."

Judy let neither his tone nor his words intimidate her. "I'll be at the door in half an hour and I'll leave with or without you. But I honestly believe that you're a man of honor."

She left the room and McFarland continued to sit at his desk, seething with frustration. She'd tricked him; she'd set him up, waited patiently and then waltzed in for the kill. His laugh was filled with bitterness. An innocent woman? He didn't think so.

Half an hour later, Judy stood in the foyer waiting for John. When he didn't come, she lingered for an additional five minutes. Deeply disappointed, she picked up the large wicker picnic basket and walked out of the house alone.

In his suite of offices, McFarland stood at the balcony door staring into space. It wasn't just that he didn't have time to spend lazing on the beach. If he truly wanted to, he could have joined her. The problem was Judy. Whenever he was with her, the need for her burned within him. A curious ache tore at his heart. Perhaps his upbringing—

or lack of one—was the problem. At no other time in his life had he wanted to know a woman the way he did Judy. He yearned to hold her in his arms and hear tales from her childhood, and tell her about his. From the little she'd described, he recognized how close she'd been to her mother. She rarely spoke of her brother or father and McFarland didn't encourage it, afraid she missed them and would ask to be released.

For his own part, McFarland had told her more of his life than he'd ever revealed to anyone. Being with her made him weak in ways he couldn't explain. That kiss was a good example. He'd promised himself he wouldn't do it and then… A low groan of frustration welled up in his throat and he momentarily closed his eyes.

Pivoting, he walked over to the liquor cabinet, poured himself a stiff drink and downed it in two swallows.

He wanted her. This soul-searching led to one thing and one thing only. He hungered to take Judy in his arms and kiss her until she felt a fraction of his desire. And when the moment came, she'd smile up at him with those incredible eyes and give him her very soul and ask nothing in return.

"Mr. McFarland?" Avery Anderson stepped into the office.

"Yes?" he snapped.

"I'm sorry to disturb you."

McFarland shook his head, dismissing the apology. "What is it?"

Avery shifted his feet. "It's Ms. Lovin."

"Yes. Is there a problem? Is she hurt?" He strove to keep his voice unemotional, although his heart was hammering anxiously against his ribs.

"No...no. Nothing like that."

"Then what?"

Avery ran a finger inside his stiff

white collar. "She's been on the island nearly a month now."

"I'm aware of that."

"I was wondering how much longer her family will be kept waiting before she's returned."

"Have they been pestering you again?" Grim resolve tightened his features. Judy enjoyed the island; he could see no reason to rush her departure.

Avery gave one barely perceptible shake of his head and dropped his gaze. "No…"

"Then who's doing the asking?"

Avery squared his shoulders and slowly raised his eyes to his employer's. "I am, sir."

"You?"

"That's right, Mr. McFarland."

"How long Ms. Lovin stays or doesn't stay is none of your concern." His tone was cold.

"But, sir…"

"That'll be all, Avery."

He hesitated for a long moment before turning, white-lipped, and walking out of the room.

McFarland watched his assistant leave. Even his staff had been cast under her spell. Sam, who could be decidedly unpleasant, rushed to do her bidding. Princess had never been groomed more frequently or better. When asked about the extra attention he'd paid to the mare, Sam had actually blushed and claimed it was for Ms. Lovin.

The maids fought to serve her. The chef had somehow managed to learn her favorite dishes and cooked them to the exclusion of all else. Pleased by his efforts, Judy had personally gone to thank him and kissed the top of his shining bald head. The island children followed her the way they would a pied piper. Even Midnight had succumbed to her considerable charm. McFarland wiped a hand over his face. The entire island rushed to fulfill her every command. Why should *he* be exempt from yearning to please her?

"Avery!" he barked.

"Sir?" The other man hurried into the room.

"Cancel my afternoon commitments."

"Excuse me?" Incredulous disbelief widened the other man's eyes.

"I said wipe out any commitments I have for the remainder of the day."

Avery checked his watch. "Are you feeling ill, Mr. McFarland? Should I contact a doctor?"

"No. I'm going swimming."

Avery's eyes narrowed. "Swimming?"

"In the ocean," McFarland said, grinning.

"The one outside—the one here?"

"That's right." Purposefully, he closed the folder on his desktop lest he be tempted to stay. "Avery, when was the last afternoon you had free?"

"I'm not sure."

"Take this one off. That's an order."

An instantaneous smile lit up the fastidious man's face. "Right away, Mr. McFarland."

McFarland felt as young as springtime and as excited as a lover on Valentine's Day. He walked through the house to his quarters and changed clothes. With a beach towel slung around his neck, he strolled down the front lawn and searched the outskirts of the beach. He found Judy lying in the shade of a tall palm tree. She wore a demure swimsuit and had kicked off her sandals. A large blanket was spread out on the grass; the picnic basket was open. He glanced inside and saw enough food to hold off a siege.

Judy lay on her back with her eyes closed. She knew she appeared tranquil, but her thoughts were spinning. She shouldn't be on St. Steven's. She should be asking when John intended to release her so she could go home to her family. Instead she was lazing on the beach feeling sorry for herself because she'd misjudged John McFarland. Her pride was hurt that he'd refused such a simple request. She liked being with John; the highlight of her day was spending time with him. She savored those minutes, and was keenly disappointed whenever he left her. The kiss they'd shared had changed everything; nothing could be the same anymore. They'd come to trust each other enough to be friends, but now they feared each other. The kiss hadn't satisfied their curiosity. Instead, it had left them yearning for more.

A soft protest sounded from her throat. She was falling in love with John. She didn't want to love him, nor did he want her love. He would hurt her and send her away when he tired of her. It would embarrass him—and her—if he ever guessed how she felt.

"You knew I'd come, didn't you?" McFarland said, standing over her.

Judy's eyes shot open, blinked at the bright sunlight and closed again. Shielding her eyes with one hand, she leaned on one elbow and looked at him again. "John." She sat upright.

He didn't seem pleased to be there, but she was too happy to care.

"Sit down." She patted the blanket beside her. "And no, I didn't know you were coming, but I'm so glad you did."

He joined her, looping an arm around his bent knee. He stared into the roll-

ing blue surf as he spoke. "I left Mc-
Donnell Douglas on the line so I could
fulfill this wager."

"They'll call you tomorrow."

"You hope."

"I know," she said, hiding a smile.
"Now don't be angry with me. You're
the one who suggested we make things
interesting."

"Why can't you be like every other
woman and ask for diamonds?"

"Because some things are worth
more than jewels."

"What's the problem? Do you have
so many that more don't interest you?"
His face was hard and unyielding, but
his anger was directed more at himself
than at Judy.

"My mother left me three or four
lovely pieces." She slowly trailed her
finger in the sand. "But I seldom wear
jewelry." He wouldn't understand and
she couldn't explain that being with

him was worth more to her than rubies and pearls.

A strained silence followed. "I shouldn't have snapped at you," he eventually said.

She turned to face him and was caught once again by his tortured gaze. Her breath stalled in her lungs. Not knowing what drove her, she brought her hand to his face, yearning to wipe away the pain. John's eyes closed as her fingers lightly brushed his cheek. He took her hand, then raised his eyes to hers, kissing the inside of her hand.

The sensation of his lips against her palm made Judy gasp.

"I shouldn't do this," he said and groaned, directing her face to his. He kissed her cheek, her temple, her eyes.

They broke apart momentarily, and when he reached for her again, Judy met him halfway. This time the kiss was much deeper, and when he lifted his head they were both dazed and more than a little shocked. The kiss was better, far better, than either had anticipated.

McFarland rose to his knees, pulling Judy with him. Her look of innocent desire stabbed at his conscience. He hadn't meant to kiss her; he feared hurting her more than he feared losing his wealth. But the soft, feminine feel of her was irresistible. And in the end, he kissed her again and again until his heart thundered and roared. He lost himself in her sweetness as years of loneliness melted away.

John's kisses made Judy feel light-headed. The finest wine couldn't produce a sensation as potent as this. She trembled in his arms and her gaze met his.

He dragged his eyes away from her.

"Let's swim," he said abruptly.

Judy nodded and he helped her to her feet.

The turquoise water wasn't far, and they stepped into the rolling surf together. The cool spray against her heated flesh took Judy's breath away.

John dove into an oncoming wave and Judy followed him. He broke the surface several feet from her, turned and waited for her to swim to him.

"Have you ever body surfed?" He shouted to be heard above the sound of the churning sea.

"No, but I'd like to."

"Good." He reached out and clasped her waist. "We'll take this wave together."

With no option, Judy closed her eyes and was thrust into the swelling wall of water. Her hold on John tightened as they were cast under the surface by a giant surge of unleashed power.

Judy threw back her head and

laughed once the wave washed them onto the beach. "That was wonderful." She wrapped her arms around John's neck.

"You're slippery," McFarland said, using the excuse to draw her closer. He held her firmly against him, his fingers brushing the wet strands of hair from her face. Her pulse went wild at his touch.

His eyes darkened just before his mouth descended on hers. Judy gave herself to the kiss, responding with all the love in her heart. The water took them again, and when they emerged from the wave, Judy was breathless and weak.

McFarland's chest heaved. He'd thought he could escape his need for her in the water, but it hadn't worked out that way. "You feel even better like this...."

"Pardon?"

"Nothing," he grumbled. How was he ever going to let her go? "Judy?"

She wound her arms around his neck and smiled shyly. Maybe he'd admit that he loved her. No, she told herself. It was a fanciful dream. Earning John's love would take more than a few playful moments in the surf. He had to learn to trust.

"Listen," he said in a low voice, "I have to tell you something."

She raised her head, afraid that he was going to send her away.

"I'm leaving."

Her heart slammed against her ribs. "When?"

"In the morning."

"How long?"

"A few days," he said, and continued to brush the wet strands from her face, although they'd long since been smoothed into place. "Four, possibly five."

Perhaps he'd decided to send her away. Her eyes must have revealed her distress.

"Will you wait here for me, Beauty?"

She nodded, overcome with relief.

"Good," he whispered, and greedily sought her mouth once again.

Not until he kissed her did she realize he hadn't called her Judy.

Six

John left just after dawn the next morning. Judy was awake and at the sound of muted voices, reached for her robe and rushed down the winding stairs. By the time she arrived, John was already gone, but she could see his Jeep in the distance. She stood on the huge porch, leaning dejectedly against the marble column. She would've liked to have wished him well.

"Morning, Ms. Lovin."

Judy straightened and turned toward Avery Anderson.

"Good morning. I see John got off without a hitch."

"Mr. McFarland should only be away a few days."

"Four, possibly five." She quoted what John had told her, staring after the disappearing vehicle. "It won't be so bad."

"He's instructed me to see to your every wish."

She smiled. If she were to have a craving for pastrami from her favorite New York deli, Judy didn't doubt that speedy arrangements would be made.

"He doesn't go away often," Avery went on to explain as he straightened his bow tie. "He wouldn't now if it wasn't necessary."

Judy nodded. John hadn't wanted to leave her. She'd seen the regret in his eyes.

"Some say he's a recluse," Avery commented thoughtfully, studying Judy.

"No," she countered. "Not in the true sense of the word, but he does care about his privacy."

"He does," the older man agreed.

They turned to go back inside, walking through the wide doors and parting at the foot of the stairs.

Four or five days wouldn't seem long, Judy told herself as she dressed. The time would fly. She glanced at her watch; already fifteen minutes had passed.

Slumping onto the edge of the bed, Judy released a long, slow breath. She loved John and was only beginning to understand the consequences of blithely handing him her heart. Caring for him excited her, and it made her afraid. John wouldn't be an easy man to love; he knew so little about it.

Judy had been surrounded by love. Her feelings for John gave him the power to hurt her and she wasn't convinced that telling him how she felt would be in her best interests—or his.

The first day passed without incident. The second was equally dull. Mealtimes were the worst. She sat at the end of the table and experienced such an overwhelming sense of loneliness that she scolded herself for being so dramatic.

Nothing seemed right without John. Not riding Princess around the island; not visiting the children; not writing letters to her family; not swimming.

She was lonely and bored, at odds with herself. One man had toppled her world and a few days without him taxed the balance of her existence.

The night of the third day, Judy tossed and turned in her bed, unable to sleep. She missed John dreadfully and was angry with herself for feeling at such a loss without him.

At midnight, she threw aside the blankets and silently crept down the stairs for a glass of milk, hoping that would help her sleep. John's office was on the opposite side of the house from the kitchen, and Judy carried her milk to the opulently paneled suite, turning on the lights. She slipped into his desk chair, tucking her bare feet beneath her. Briefly she closed her eyes and smiled, inhaling his scent. She could practically feel his presence, and that eased the ache of loneliness and despair.

Weary to the bone, McFarland entered the house and paused in the foyer, resisting the urge to climb the stairs and wake Judy. The thought of holding her sleepy head against his chest was almost more than he could resist.

The business meetings hadn't gone well and in part he blamed himself. Negotiations had come to an impasse and, in his impatience to return to the island, he'd asked that the meeting be adjourned while both parties considered the lengthy proposals. He would've stayed in Dallas if he'd felt it would do any good, but he figured it was probably better to return to St. Steven's rather than buckle under to United Petroleum's unreasonable demands.

He paused, rubbed a hand over his face and smiled. He didn't need to wake Judy to feel her presence in his home. He had only to shut his eyes to see her bouncing down the stairs with a vitality that rivaled life itself. Her laughter was like sparkling water; her smile could blot out the sun.

His heart constricted with emotion. He would surprise her first thing in the morning. Until then he'd have to be content.

With that in mind, he headed toward his rooms, until a light in his office attracted his attention. It wasn't like Avery to work this late unless there was a major problem. Frowning, McFarland decided to check.

One step into his office and he stopped cold. Judy was curled up in the chair behind his desk, sound asleep. She was the picture of innocence with her head to one side, the thick coffee-colored hair falling over her cheek. She wore a plain nightgown beneath an equally unfeminine robe. Neither did much to reveal the womanly curves beneath. However, McFarland had never experienced a stronger stab of desire. It cut through him, sharp and intense, and trapped the breath in his lungs.

Had it been any other woman, he would've kissed her awake, then carried her into his room and satisfied his yearning. He couldn't do that with Judy; her innocence prevented him.

He hesitated, debating how he should wake her. His impulse, despite everything, was to bend over and kiss her, but he knew that would never satisfy him and the potency of his desire would only shock her. Shaking her or calling her name might frighten her.

Of her own accord, Judy stirred and stretched her arms above her head, arching her back and yawning loudly. She hadn't meant to fall asleep. When she opened her eyes, she discovered John standing on the other side of the desk. She blinked. At first she was convinced he wasn't real but the embodiment of her deepest desires. When she realized he was actually there, she leaped from the chair, nearly tripping on the hem of her nightgown.

"John." She brought her hand to her

chest. "I'm so sorry…I don't know what came over me to come into your office. It must've startled you to find me here. I…I apologize."

"My home is yours. No apology is necessary," he said softly as his gaze fell on the empty glass.

"I couldn't sleep." She shook back her hair, still flustered and more than a little embarrassed. "When did you get in?"

He felt a smile twitch at the corners of his mouth. She looked like a guilty child with her hand in the cookie jar. "A few minutes ago."

She clasped her hands and smiled brightly. "Welcome home."

"It's good to be here."

Judy tightened her hands to restrain the urge to run into his arms, hold on to him and beg him never to leave her again. Her heart continued to pound, but she didn't know if it was from being caught in his office or just the sight of him.

"Did anything happen while I was away?" he asked, reaching for his mail and idly flipping through it.

"Nothing important." She stood across from him, drinking in his presence as though he might disappear at any moment. "Are you hungry? I'd be happy to fix you something." She prayed he was famished, so she'd have an excuse to stay with him longer.

"Don't go to any trouble."

"I won't. Will a sandwich do?" She smiled, inordinately pleased to be able to do this one small thing for him.

"A sandwich would be fine."

He followed her into the kitchen and pulled a stool up to the stainless-steel table while Judy opened the refrigerator to take out the necessary ingredients.

"How was the trip?" she asked, liberally slathering two slices of bread with mayonnaise before placing turkey and tomato on them.

McFarland had never discussed business matters with anyone outside his office. The temptation to do it now was strong, but he didn't. "Everything went as expected," he said matter-of-factly, which was only half true.

Judy cut the sandwich in half, set it on a plate and handed it to him. She poured them each a glass of milk, then sat on a stool across from him.

Elbows braced on the table, she cupped her face in her hands and studied him while he ate. Her brow creased with concern. "You look exhausted."

"I am. I didn't make it to bed last night."

"The meetings didn't go well, did they?"

Her intuition surprised him; he

hadn't thought he was that easy to read. "I didn't expect them to."

"What happened?"

McFarland shrugged. "I made an offer, they rejected it and came back with a counteroffer."

"And you rejected that?"

He paused, the glass halfway to his mouth. "Not exactly. Not yet, anyway," he elaborated.

"But you will?"

Again he shrugged, and his eyes met hers. "I'm not sure."

Judy continued to study John. He was physically exhausted, but his mental stress weighed far more heavily on him. As a young girl, she'd often watched her mother soothe away her father's tension. Georgia Lovin hadn't made suggestions; she'd had no expertise in business, but she possessed the ability to get her husband to relax and talk out the problem. More often than not, he found the solution. Judy prayed she could do the same for John.

"You want this deal, don't you?" she asked him softly.

McFarland nodded. "I've been working on it for over a year. The offer I made United Petroleum is a fair one— it was more than fair. But I'm at a disadvantage."

"Why?"

He set the glass down hard. "Because they know I want this."

"I see."

"Now that you mention it, I may have appeared too anxious to settle." He couldn't deny his eagerness. He'd wanted to get those papers signed so he could get back to the island and Judy, his mission accomplished. He'd thought he'd been more subtle, but perhaps not. "Let me explain," he said, taking a napkin and scribbling down a series of figures.

He spoke nonstop for fifteen minutes. Much of what he said was beyond Judy's comprehension, although she pretended to understand every bit of it. She nodded at the appropriate times, occasionally asking a question, and smiled when he finished.

"You're right," he said with a wide grin. "Why didn't I think of that?"

Judy understood only some of what he was talking about, but it didn't seem to matter. The weariness was gone from his eyes. He stood and paced the kitchen.

"That's it," he said, pausing in front of her. "Has anyone ever told you what a marvel you are?" His hands cradled her face and he kissed her soundly.

Judy's breath lodged in her chest. "What was that for?"

"To thank you." He checked his watch. "It's late, but I think I'll call my attorney and talk this latest strategy over with him."

"John," she protested. "It's one o'clock in the morning!"

"For the money I pay that man it shouldn't make any difference what time I call him."

Before she could protest further, John was at the kitchen door. He opened it, paused and turned back. "Will you ride with me in the morning?"

She smiled and nodded eagerly, grateful that he'd asked.

In his office, McFarland emptied his briefcase and set the file for United Petroleum on his desk. It struck him then, sharply. He didn't know how, but Judy had gotten him to reveal the minute details of this buyout. He'd told her everything without any hesitation. He wasn't worried about what she'd do with the information; there *was* nothing she could do.

But he was shocked by the way she'd so completely gained his confidence—to the point that he cheerfully gave out industry secrets without a second thought. This woman had him tied in knots a sailor couldn't untangle, and every one of them was choking off his independence. Because she was making herself essential.

He paused as he analyzed the situation. McFarland didn't like the idea of a woman, any woman, controlling his life. Not one bit. Something had to be done to put an end to it.

At dawn Judy rushed to meet John at the stables. She'd slept well after leaving him. When the maid had come to wake her, she'd resisted climbing out of the warm bed, preferring to hold on to the memory of John's arms around her. It took her a moment to realize she'd been dreaming.

Midnight and Princess were saddled and waiting.

"Morning," she called to Sam and smiled at John, who immediately swung onto Midnight's back.

The burly trainer waved. Judy stroked Princess's smooth neck before mounting. She noticed that John's look remained stoic.

"How'd you sleep?" she asked when they'd gone a few hundred feet. He was quiet, withdrawn and taciturn—nothing like the warm, gentle man he'd been when they'd parted.

"I didn't get to bed," he answered crisply.

"Oh, John, again? You must be ready to fall out of the saddle."

"No. After you left last night, I started to analyze the proposal and decided there were still things I wanted to change before I talked to Butterman."

Judy assumed Butterman was his attorney. "What did he have to say?"

John's expression was thoughtful. "Not much. But he seemed to think the new strategy would work. Unless United Petroleum wants to play games, I should hear back sometime this afternoon." He tipped back the brim of his hat and glanced at his watch. "The fact is, I should probably cut our ride short and get back to the office in case they contact me this morning."

Judy was aghast. "You don't intend to work, do you? Good heavens, you've been away on an exhausting business trip."

"So?"

"You haven't slept in who knows how long!"

McFarland's mouth thinned. "What's that got to do with anything?"

"Everything," she cried, losing her own temper. She didn't know what was wrong with him, but she had a hunch that a few hours' rest would cure it.

"Just what am I supposed to do?"

"Sleep."

"I'm expecting a phone call."

"Avery will wake you."

"What are you? My nurse?"

Judy's gloved hands tightened around the reins at the harsh edge to his voice. "Someone needs to look after you."

"And you're volunteering for the job?" McFarland didn't want to shout at her, but he couldn't seem to make himself stop. She was right. He hadn't seen a bed in over forty-eight hours, but he sure didn't want a woman dictating his actions.

Judy clamped her mouth shut, refusing to rise to the bait.

They rode together for half an hour without saying a word. McFarland derived little pleasure from the outing.

He regretted having snapped at Judy, especially when he would much rather have taken her in his arms and kissed her. He searched for a way to apologize without losing his pride, and found none.

When they'd returned to the stable, Judy lowered herself from Princess's back and turned toward John. "As I recall, only a few hours ago you considered me wise and insightful. I don't know what happened since then, but I really do wish you'd rest."

"Why?"

She clenched her fists. "You're killing yourself working day and night for no reason."

"I call a hundred million dollars a damn good reason."

"Is it worth your health?" she cried, tears glistening in her eyes. "Is it worth becoming so unreasonable no one can even talk to you? Is it worth saying things you don't mean?"

"You seem to be doing exactly that."

"No. I mean everything I say." She paused. "I care about you."

"Is that supposed to excite me?" he asked. "You care about everything— horses, children...bugs. It would be hard to find something you *didn't* care about. Listen, Miss Bleeding Heart, I can do without your meddling. Got that?"

"No," she said with pride, her face pale and grim.

"You've been nothing but a nuisance since you came to the island. There isn't a man or woman here who doesn't bend to your every wish. Well, I refuse to be one of them. You'll do what I tell you. It won't be the other way around. Is that clear?"

If possible, her face went even paler, and her eyes widened with unmistakable pain. She opened her mouth to say something, then closed it again. But she refused to look away.

"I won't bother you again, John Mc-Farland," she whispered with quiet dignity and turned away from him. How quickly everything had changed. She'd missed John desperately. She'd longed to savor this morning's outing with him and instead had been subjected to an outburst she didn't understand.

In her rooms, she sat and stared at the wall as the tears began to flow down her cheeks. She was in love with a beast. The possibility of ever gaining his heart struck her as ludicrous. In his own words, she was a nuisance and, with that, Judy realized that he'd probably never be capable of loving her.

At lunchtime, she sent a message that she wouldn't be joining him and requested that all her meals be sent to her room. If John found her company so taxing, there was no need to punish him with it. She was determined to avoid him until he saw fit to summon her.

A day passed.

A night.

Another day.

Another long, sleepless night.

A third day came and went, and still John didn't ask for her. She thought about him, yearned for him. She loved him and he considered her an annoyance. All these weeks when she'd treasured every moment with him, he'd seen her as a bother, a pest.

Still, he didn't summon her. To escape her rooms, Judy walked along the beach in the early morning. For the first time in weeks she entertained thoughts of leaving, but ultimately rejected them. They'd struck a bargain, and although it became increasingly difficult, she would stay on the island until he sent her away.

Countless times Judy wondered why he kept her there. She yearned to be with her family.

McFarland was not amused by Judy's stubbornness. Perhaps he'd been a bit unreasonable, but her reaction was even more so. For four days, she'd refused to have anything to do with him. That had been her choice, but enough was enough. The entire house was in an uproar.

Earlier McFarland had discovered the chef arguing with Avery. French insults gushed like water out of a spigot while the four-star chef gestured freely with his hands. The entire time, the man glanced accusingly in McFarland's direction.

"What was that all about?" he'd asked his assistant later.

"He—ah—is concerned," Avery commented, looking embarrassed.

"Concerned? Is there a problem with the kitchen staff?"

"No." Avery busied himself shifting papers around his desk.

"Then what is it?"

"He's concerned about Ms. Lovin."

McFarland's grin faded and his eyes grew cold. "Judy? What's wrong?"

"He claims she isn't eating properly and that she sends back her meals untouched. He's tempted her with his most famous recipes and nothing seems to work. He's afraid she's making herself ill."

A muscle jerked convulsively in McFarland's clenched jaw.

"I realize this isn't any of my business, Mr. McFarland, but…"

"You're right. It isn't."

Avery squared his shoulders, his own jaw tightening. "I've been with you for several years now, but these last three days have been the most difficult. You've been impatient and unreasonably demanding, and I can see no excuse for it. You have my notice, Mr. McFarland."

McFarland was stunned. Perhaps he *had* been a bit more demanding in the past few days, but that wasn't any reason for Avery to resign. "As you wish," he answered with some reluctance.

The afternoon went smoothly after that, but when they'd finished, Avery presented him with a brief but precise letter of resignation.

McFarland read it over twice, convinced there must've been some mistake. There wasn't; Avery was leaving him.

In an effort to think through this unexpected turn of events, McFarland got two cold beers and decided to visit Sam. To his additional shock, he discovered that the stableman regarded him with a black scowl.

"Don't tell me she's got you on her side, as well?" McFarland barked, angry because he should've known better. She'd had Sam twisted around her little finger from the minute she'd tamed Midnight. "Doesn't even one of you recognize the hand that feeds you? I don't believe it. Not you, too?"

In response, Sam chuckled, ambled to the back of the barn and brought out two rickety chairs.

"Women aren't worth the trouble they cause," McFarland said, pulling the tab from the aluminum top and guzzling a long swallow.

Sam joined him in the toast. "Can't say I blame you. You'd do well to be rid of her."

McFarland wiped his mouth with the back of his hand. "What do you mean?"

"You don't plan to keep her on the island? Not with the way she's been acting."

McFarland planned exactly that. He had no intention of letting her leave. She was there of her own free will— at any rate, she'd chosen to come. This disagreement between them was a spat, nothing more. She'd infringed on his private life and he wouldn't stand for it. Given time, she'd acknowledge that and she'd apologize and the situation would return to the way it used to be.

"She's a busybody, that one," Sam added. "Why, look at the way she stuck her nose in your affairs, dictating how you should run your business. No man should be expected to put up with that kind of intrusion."

McFarland nodded slowly, a little taken aback by Sam's vehemence.

"Look at the way she's always needling you, making one demand after another. I hear she constantly wants gifts."

McFarland shook his head. "She's never asked for a thing. Not for herself, anyway."

Sam took a swallow of beer. "If I were you, I'd put her in a rowboat and cast her out of my life. Let her fend for herself. As you said, she's a nuisance. She isn't worth the trouble."

McFarland mumbled something unintelligible. "Who said she was a nuisance?"

"You did! I heard you tell her so myself. You should've seen the look in her eyes." Sam's laugh was loud and boisterous. "She's full of pride and spirit, that one. You'd better break it if you intend to keep her around."

"What else did I say to her?"

"Oh, lots of things."

"What things?"

McFarland felt sick as Sam told him.

He'd been so exhausted that he didn't remember half of it. Now, every word, every syllable, was like a vicious punch to his abdomen.

McFarland crushed the aluminum can with his hands and stood.

"Where are you going?"

He didn't answer.

"You're going to get rid of her, aren't you?" Sam asked, and noting the expression on McFarland's face, he chuckled, pleased with himself.

A little reverse psychology wouldn't go amiss, Sam figured. It worked with stubborn horses. Why not their owners?

Seven

Once again McFarland was in the uncomfortable position of having to seek Judy's forgiveness. His behavior gnawed at his conscience and wouldn't let him sleep. He rolled over and stared at the darkened ceiling. His heart constricted and his first serious doubts concerning what he was doing with Judy began to surface. He'd seen her picture in some newspaper and his interest had been awakened. He didn't quite understand what craziness had driven him to bring her to his island. In the weeks since her arrival, his life had been drastically affected. She'd been open, happy, guileless and un-believably gentle when she had every excuse to hate him. He'd berated her, lashed out at her and still she turned those beautiful eyes on him and man-aged to smile.

By everything that was right, he should send her back to her family. His heart pounded slowly, painfully, at the thought of never hearing the sound of her laughter again, or having those eyes smile into his, or seeing her ride across his land with her hair in disar-ray. A heaviness weighed on his chest.

He couldn't do it—sending her away was unthinkable. The tenderness in her eyes and her smile filled him with an exhilaration he couldn't analyze. He wasn't even sure he wanted to. She made him feel things he'd never experienced, emotions he'd fought against most of his life. All he knew was that he needed her on St. Steven's for now. He'd deal with tomorrow later.

Judy punched her pillow and battled another wave of depression. She was wide awake. With nothing better to do, she climbed out of bed, dressed and crept out of the house, heading for the stables.

She felt incredibly weary.

The sky remained dark, but the promise of dawn lay just over the horizon. She could hear Sam stirring in the back of the barn as she saddled Princess and rode toward the beach.

Sam's features were twisted in a scowl as he searched McFarland's face in the half light of early dawn.

"She's gone," he announced harshly.

"Who?" McFarland stood beside

Midnight, already saddled and waiting for him.

"Princess."

McFarland's eyes widened. No one would dare steal the mare. Only Judy rode her. "Has anyone checked the house to see—"

"The maid says there's no one in her room. Her bed barely looks slept in."

McFarland's own features hardened with determination, and in a single motion, he swung his weight onto Midnight's back. "What direction does she usually take?"

Sam gestured widely with both hands. "North. Sometimes east."

"I'll head west."

Sam's nod was curt, his eyes boring into McFarland's. "You bring her back. She belongs here."

McFarland raced out of the yard. He wouldn't come back until he found her. He'd punish whoever had helped her in this underhanded scheme. What good was security if she could carry out her own escape? He'd fire the lot of them, but first he had to find Judy.

McFarland would've ridden from one side of the island to the other, torn down the entire jungle to stop her. To his utter astonishment, all it took was a wild fifteen-minute ride. He came upon her with such ease that his heart began to slam against his chest. He paused, his frantic heartbeat stilling as he raised his eyes in gratitude.

She was walking on the beach with Princess following behind. The reins were draped over her shoulders as she ambled along. Although McFarland was high on the ridge above, he could see how distressed Judy was. Her head hung low, her shoulders were hunched and she moved slowly, despondently. He didn't need to see her tear-streaked face to know she'd been crying. That realization had the oddest effect on him. Guilt overwhelmed him and his chest constricted with a pain that was razor sharp. He couldn't take his eyes off her. Witnessing her sorrow brought such an intense desire to protect her that he could hardly breathe.

Since the night Sam had told him about the things he'd said to Judy, McFarland had sought a means of apologizing while salvaging his pride. He could give her a token gift, perhaps. Something that would convey his message without costing him emotionally. Watching her now, a sick feeling settled in the pit of his stomach and he admitted that he'd gladly fall to his knees and beg her forgiveness. He was a selfish bastard and Beauty—his Beauty—deserved so much better.

Judy wiped the tears from her cheeks, angry with herself for being

so melancholy. From the first, she'd
known it would be difficult to love
John. She'd thought she had accepted
that. In the long days since their ride
together, she'd come to understand the
cost that love demanded. But she had
her pride, too—in some ways it was
as great as John's—and she would die
before she'd let him know that he held
her heart in the palm of his hand.

A flash of ebony caught her attention and she turned and spotted John
on the ridge above her. He pulled on
the reins and she realized with a start
that he was planning to meet her. It
was one thing to know he'd found her,
and another to let him see her tears.

Frantic to escape, she mounted Princess and slapped the reins hard. The
mare shot across the beach, kicking
up a flurry of sand. Judy decided her
best chance of escape was the jungle
and went in that direction. Risking a

look behind her, she was astonished to see that John had already arrived at the beach.

"Hurry, Princess," she cried as the horse charged ahead.

Judy didn't see what darted across the beach, but Princess reared, her front legs kicking in terror. Unable to stop herself, Judy slipped sideways in the saddle. She made a desperate effort to regain her balance, but it was too difficult to stay on the bucking horse. A sense of unreality filled her. She hadn't been thrown by a horse since she was a child. She refused to believe it, but the ground that rushed up to meet her was certainly real. With a cry of panic she put out her arms to break the fall. Then the impact of her body against the beach brutally drove the air from her lungs.

McFarland saw Princess buck and watched helplessly as Judy teetered, frantically trying to regain her seat. He saw her fall and knew she'd landed hard. Swearwords scorched the morning mist and his heart thundered with alarm. The thoughts that flashed through his mind were completely illogical. He'd sell his business interests around the world if she was unhurt. If that didn't satisfy the powers that be, he offered his life, his soul—anything—as long as Judy wasn't hurt.

He pulled Midnight to an abrupt halt, vaulted from the stallion's back and ran across the sand, more frightened than he could remember ever being.

Falling to his knees at Judy's side, he gently rolled her over. The steady, even pulsing at the side of her neck made him go weak with relief. He yanked off his jacket and placed it under her head. Then, not knowing what else to do, he held her limp hand in his own, rubbing the inside of her wrist.

Judy's eyes fluttered open to see John leaning over her, looking sickly pale. "Princess?" she whispered and tried to sit up.

It took McFarland a moment to realize she was worried about the mare. He was astonished; Judy could have been maimed, or worse, killed, and she seemed to care nothing for her own well-being.

"Is she hurt?"

McFarland shook his head and responded in a husky voice. "She's fine. She's already on her way back to the stable. What about you? How do you feel?"

Her smile was little more than a slight trembling of her lips. It was too soon to tell. She felt like she might throw up and the world spun crazily. "I'm all right," she said weakly.

"You're sure?" His eyes burned into hers.

"The only thing bruised is my pride." With some difficulty she stood, then stumbled and swayed toward him. Her ribs hurt badly, but she successfully hid the pain.

McFarland caught her, wrapping his arms around her, holding her against him, grateful for the excuse to bring her into his embrace. He brushed her disheveled hair away from her face, and Judy noted that he was shaking as much as she was.

"I'm fine, John. Something must have spooked Princess. I think it was a rabbit." She tilted her head back and saw the torment in his expression as he relived the moment of her fall.

Their eyes met. Neither moved; neither breathed. Slowly, he lowered his mouth to hers. Judy could find no way to describe the turbulent sensations that jolted her. It was as though she realized she could've been killed and forever denied the feel of John's arms around her. Judy wanted to cherish this moment forever and forget the pain.

They remained locked in each other's arms long after the kiss had ended. Timeless seconds passed, each more precious than the one before.

"You have to see a doctor," he said at last.

"John, I'll be fine."

"You're shaking."

She smiled, unable to tell him his kisses contributed to her trembling as much as the pain.

His low whistle brought Midnight to their side. "You'll ride with me."

"But…"

One look cut off any argument. McFarland climbed into Midnight's saddle first.

Judy stared at the stallion and felt her knees go weak. The last thing she wanted to do right now was get back on a horse. Although she strove to reassure John that she was unhurt, she felt as though someone had taken a baseball bat to her ribs. It hurt to breathe and she ached everywhere. Nothing seemed broken, but something wasn't right, either. "What if he won't let me?" she asked shakily.

John dismissed the idea with a curious smile. "You said yourself that Midnight is your friend."

She nodded, staring at the hand he offered her. She took it, and his strong fingers closed over hers as he prepared to lift her onto the stallion's back. However, the simple act of raising her arm caused her to gasp with pain.

Hurriedly, she drew it back to her side, closed her eyes and pressed her forehead against John's leg. The next thing she knew, she was on her knees in the sand, clutching her side.

"You idiot!" he shouted, dismounting. "Why didn't you say something?"

Tears welled in her eyes as she lifted her gaze to his. "Why do you always yell at me?" she asked in a hoarse whisper.

"Beauty, I'm sorry."

She held her arm protectively across her ribs. "Only my father calls me that."

"It's true, you know," he said, kneeling beside her, holding her with such tenderness that she couldn't identify the greater pain—loving John or the ache in her ribs.

"I'm not beautiful."

"Yes, you are. You're the most beautiful woman I know. Now don't argue with me anymore."

She gave him a weak smile.

The trip back to the house was torture and seemed to take hours. She pleaded with him to leave her there and send someone back for her. The injury wasn't so bad that she couldn't stand to be alone for half an hour. John adamantly refused and, in the end, she did ride Midnight, cradled in John's arms.

She rode facing him, her head against his chest, her arms around his middle. Their progress was slow and by the time they arrived she was hazy with pain and incredibly sleepy.

Sam and several others rushed out to greet them.

"Send for a doctor," John shouted urgently. That meant flying one in, which would take time, but there was no alternative.

With some effort, Judy lifted her head. "I thought you weren't going to yell anymore."

"I said that?" He pretended to be surprised.

She frowned and drew in a slow, painful breath. "Maybe you didn't."

He buried his fingers in her hair. "If it'll make the hurt go away," he whispered, "I promise never to raise my voice again."

The ache in her side immediately lessened.

He issued other orders, but in a subdued voice that moved her deeply, not because she found his shouting objectionable, but because he cared enough to try to please her. After the last four days of the bitter war that had raged between them, this sweet attention was bliss.

John helped her off Midnight and carried her into the house. She protested when he started up the stairs to her room, but it didn't stop him.

"I'm too heavy," she cried.

"Now look who's yelling."

"John, please, you're the one who'll need a doctor if you insist on hauling me up these stairs."

"I'll risk it."

"I wish you wouldn't." But it was useless to protest. Besides, he was already halfway up the stairs.

When he reached the hallway outside her suite, he nudged her door open, crossed the room and placed her carefully on the bed. Judy immediately recognized that lying down wasn't the thing to do and, kicking out her feet, she struggled to a sitting position.

"What's wrong?" McFarland saw the flash of pain in her eyes and felt it as strongly as if the agony were his own.

She shook her head and closed her eyes. "Nothing. Just go away, please. I'll be fine in a minute."

To her surprise he did leave her, but two maids were in her room within seconds. They were followed by the security guard who'd met her the day of her arrival.

Judy grinned. "So we meet again."

"I have some medical training," he explained. "Mr. McFarland asked that I check you over before the doctor gets here."

Judy nodded and slumped onto the end of her bed.

McFarland was pacing in the hallway outside her room when Wilson returned. "Well?" he asked anxiously.

"My guess is that she's cracked a couple of ribs."

"She's in considerable pain, isn't she?" Although Judy tried to hide it from him, McFarland could tell that she wanted to scream and once again he felt her agony.

"She's pretending it doesn't hurt, but I know better," Wilson said wryly.

"Give her something for the pain," McFarland demanded gruffly.

The other man looked uncertain. "I don't know if I should, Mr. McFarland. The doctor might want to—"

"It could be hours before he shows up. Give her something and do it now. That's an order."

Wilson nodded, swallowing any argument. "Right away."

He returned a few minutes later with two capsules, instructing Judy to take both. Within minutes she drifted into a troubled sleep. She lay tightly curled up, taking shallow breaths, trying to minimize the pain.

When she woke, she discovered John sitting at her bedside, staring at his hands, his face bleak.

"John?"

He straightened and turned toward her. "Yes, Beauty?"

"The island needs…something. A medical facility. What if one of the children gets hurt? Then…what? There's nowhere…" She felt so sluggish, so miserable. The pills hadn't taken the away pain; only her mind was numb.

"The doctor will be here soon," he assured her.

She nodded and moistened her lips with her tongue. "I'm thirsty."

"Here." He lifted her head and held a glass of cool water to her lips. She managed to take several sips. When she'd finished, he kissed her forehead.

"John?" Her voice was a slurred whisper. She struggled to keep her eyes open, but gave up the effort.

The catch in her voice stabbed at his heart. "Yes?"

"I'm sorry I've been such a nuisance."

The words burned him like a red-hot iron. "You were never a nuisance."

"But you said—"

He gripped her hand in his own and raised it to his lips, kissing her knuckles.

"I was wrong." McFarland couldn't remember ever admitting that to anyone.

He stayed at her bedside until the medical team arrived. Then he lingered outside her room until the physician had completed his examination, which seemed to take hours. McFarland paced the area in front of her room for so long that he grew dizzy.

His thoughts mingled with each other until they dashed through his mind in a muddled sequence. Judy running away from him, Judy falling, Judy in pain. It was all his fault.

When the physician finally did appear, McFarland found himself studying the other man, fearing what he might learn. "Will she be all right?" His eyes pleaded with the white-haired man for assurance.

"I believe so. We brought along a portable X-ray machine. She's cracked two ribs and has a slight concussion."

"Any internal damage?" That was McFarland's greatest fear.

"Not that we can detect."

He jerked his fingers through his hair. "Should she be hospitalized?"

The physician shook his head. "I don't see how that would do any good. What she needs now more than *anything* is rest. For the time being she isn't going to feel like getting out of bed. However, that's for the best. Let her sleep."

"How long?"

"A couple of days. After that, she should gradually increase her activity."

"What about the pain? I don't want her to suffer." He couldn't bear to see her face twisted in agony.

"I've left some medication with my nurse, Ms. Reinholt. Ms. Lovin is sleeping comfortably now."

McFarland let out his breath in a long, slow sigh. "Good. Thank you, doctor." He offered the physician his hand and had Wilson escort the medical team to the waiting helicopter. Except for the nurse, who'd be staying as long as necessary.

McFarland checked on Judy one last time before going to his office. He was stalled in the foyer by several of the staff members. They raised questioning eyes to him, their concern evident.

"How is Judy—Ms. Lovin—sir?" the chef asked as he bravely stepped forward.

Only hours earlier McFarland would've bitten off the man's head for daring to approach him on a subject that was none of his business. Now he patiently explained the extent of Judy's injuries and answered a legion of questions.

From there McFarland went to his offices. Avery stood when he entered the room.

Before his assistant could ask, he rattled off his now-rehearsed report. "Cracked ribs, bruises and a mild concussion. She'll be confined to her bed for a few days and good as new in a couple of months. Or so the doctor says."

Avery nodded. "How about you?"

"Me?"

"It doesn't appear to me that *you're* going to recover in a couple of months," he said boldly.

McFarland glared at his assistant before walking into his office and soundly closing the door. Avery was right; McFarland doubted he'd ever be the same. He'd been shaken to the very core of his existence. He buried his face in his hands and sat, unmoving, for what felt like hours.

Somehow he made it through the day, dictating memos, making decisions, charting the course of numerous companies, but for all the emotion he put into it, he could've been playing Monopoly. Nothing seemed real; nothing seemed right.

The mere thought of food nauseated him. He couldn't eat, couldn't work. And when night came, he discovered that he couldn't sleep, either. He'd tried to stay away, to let her rest, and realized it was impossible.

The nurse in the stiff white uniform answered his knock at Judy's door.

"She's sleeping."

McFarland nodded, feeling foolish. "Go ahead and take a break. I'll stay with her."

The woman looked grateful and left soon afterward.

McFarland was thankful to spend the time alone with Judy. Her face was relaxed and revealed no signs of pain, which eased the guilt that had burdened him from the moment he'd watched Judy fall helplessly to the ground.

He couldn't tolerate the thought of her in pain. He wasn't squeamish, never had been, but Judy's accident had terrified him. He'd gone weak. With others, McFarland often battled feelings of rage; with Judy he could only blame himself. He felt sick with guilt.

"John." His name was a faint whisper.

"I'm here." Anxiously, he brought the chair closer to her bedside.

The clock on the nightstand said it was near midnight. Or was it noon? Judy didn't know anymore. Everything was so unclear. "Have you been here all this time?"

"No." He shook his head. "The nurse needed a break."

"The nurse?"

"Yes, the doctor felt you needed

round-the-clock attention for a little while."

"That's ridiculous." She tried to laugh and sucked in a breath, her ribs protesting.

"Shh, you're supposed to keep quiet."

She ignored that and pushed herself up on one elbow. "Help me sit up, would you?"

"No."

"John, please, I need to talk to you."

"No, you don't."

"I'm on my deathbed, remember? Humor me."

He grudgingly helped her into a sitting position. Next he fluffed up her pillow and tucked the sheets securely around her waist.

A smile lit up her eyes and for the life of him, McFarland couldn't tear his gaze away. "There," he said, proudly, brushing his palms against each other as though he'd accomplished some impressive feat.

"What's that?" Judy pointed at a small crate on the floor next to the dresser.

"A gift."

"From whom?"

"Me."

Although it required some effort, she managed a smile. "Well, for heaven's sake, bring it to me."

He took it from the crate after breaking off the strips of wood. It was cradled in a thick blanket. "I meant to have it wrapped, but…"

"Oh, John, it doesn't matter. As it is, I don't really know why you'd want to buy me anything."

The room went quiet as McFarland reclaimed his chair. "Go ahead and open it."

The object was heavy and awkward

in her lap. With infinite care, Judy unrolled the blanket, her excitement growing. As the bronze figure was gradually revealed, she raised her eyes to his. "John? Oh, John, could this be what I think it is?"

He arched both eyebrows playfully. "I don't know."

Tears filled her eyes and Judy bit her lip, too overcome to speak.

"Judy?"

She pressed her fingers to her mouth as she blinked back the tears. "It's the Riordan sculpture Mother gave Father. He was forced to sell it...recently."

"Yes."

"You knew?" Her hand lovingly traced the bronze, stroking it as though she hadn't believed she'd ever hold it in her hands again.

Reverently, she set the sculpture aside and lifted her arms to John. Tears shone in her eyes. "Come here," she whispered brokenly. "I want to thank you."

Eight

McFarland made excuses to visit
Judy. Ten times a day he found reasons that demanded he go to her. He
discovered it was necessary to confer
with her nurse at least twice a day. He
delivered Judy's lunch along with his
own so they could share their meals. In
the evening, he felt Ms. Reinholt, the
nurse, should have some time off, so
McFarland took it upon himself to stay
with the patient. Seldom did he come
empty-handed. Judy's injury was the

perfect excuse to give her the things he felt she deserved.

Judy's eyes would light up with such happiness at his arrival that his excuses became flimsier with every day. The Riordan sculpture rested on the nightstand and more than once McFarland had caught Judy gazing at it longingly. He knew the piece reminded her of her life in New York, but she never mentioned leaving the island. Neither did he.

"John," Judy whispered the third day of her convalescence. "You have to send that woman home." She bobbed her head in the direction of the stiff-backed nurse who sat knitting in the opposite corner of the room.

"Why?" He lowered his voice conspiratorially, his eyes twinkling.

"I'm not joking, so quit laughing at me! Ms. Reinholt is driving me crazy. Every time I turn around she's flashing a light in my eyes or sticking a thermometer under my tongue. When I complained, she suggested there were other places she could stick the blasted thing."

Despite himself, McFarland burst into laughter.

Judy's eyes narrowed and she whispered, "I'm glad you consider this so amusing."

"I'm sorry," he said, but he didn't feel at all contrite.

In a huff, Judy crossed her arms over her chest and tried to be angry with him. She couldn't. He'd been so wonderful, so attentive, that it wasn't possible to find fault with him. It was as though he yearned to make up to her for his harshness since her arrival on the island.

"I'm tired of sitting in bed." She tried to appear stern, but the edges of her mouth quivered with suppressed laughter.

He grinned.

"You'd think I was the only woman who'd ever survived two cracked ribs, the way everyone's acting. Well, I've got news for you. I am not a medical marvel."

"I realize that."

"No, you don't," she said. "Otherwise you'd let me get up."

"You are allowed to get up."

"Sure, for five minutes every hour. Big deal." She thrust out her arm. "I'm losing my tan! I'll have you know I worked hard for this."

He chuckled, and Judy resisted the urge to poke her elbow into his ribs.

"You aren't taking me seriously, John!"

"All right, all right. I'll tell Ms. Reinholt you can get up more often."

"I want to sit in the sun," she pleaded.

"Perhaps tomorrow."

There was no point in arguing. "Promise?"

He nodded. His eyes held hers and were so warm and caressing that Judy wondered why she longed for sunshine when she had John.

"And…"

"Hmm?"

"No more gifts." Her room was filled to overflowing with everything he'd given her. There was hardly space for all the flowers—roses, orchids, daisies. In addition, he'd given her bottle upon bottle of expensive perfume, and box after box of jewelry until she swore she could open her own store. Her slightest wish had been fulfilled ten times over.

"I like giving you things."

Her hand reached for his. Intuitively Judy recognized that John was soothing his conscience. She frowned; it was important that he know she didn't blame him. "The accident wasn't your fault."

His fingers tightened on hers. "I caused you to fall…"

"John, no." Her free hand stroked his clenched jaw. "I was the one who ran from you. It was an accident." In her opinion, the pain of cracked ribs was a small price to pay for an end to the hostility between them.

Ms. Reinholt set her knitting aside and checked her watch. "It's time to take Ms. Lovin's temperature," she said crisply.

"See what I mean?" Judy muttered.

"I'd better get back to the office." John leaned over and lightly brushed his lips over hers, then stood and left the room.

Obediently, Judy opened her mouth as the nurse approached. She lay back and closed her eyes, savoring the memory of those moments with John. Although he came often, he seldom stayed more than ten or fifteen minutes. Judy was so pleased to see him for any amount of time that she didn't complain.

John wasn't her only visitor. Avery Anderson arrived shortly after noon, pulled up a chair and talked for an hour. He was a fussy man, not much taller than she was and couldn't seem to finish a sentence without stuttering. She found him oddly charming, though, and toward the end of their conversation, he seemed to relax.

Ten minutes after Avery's visit, John reappeared, looking perplexed. He ran his fingers through his hair and studied her. "What did you say to Avery?"

"When?"

"Just now. He was here, wasn't he?"

Judy nodded. "I didn't say anything special. He came to see how I was doing. You don't mind, do you? I mean, if he should've been doing something else, I apologize."

John shook his head absently. "We'd finished for the day."

"What's wrong, then?"

"Nothing." John smiled then, a rich, rare smile. "He's decided to stay."

"Avery? I didn't know he was leaving."

"He isn't," John said. "At least, not anymore."

"I'm glad."

He stared at her. "You're sure you didn't say anything?"

"I said a lot of things."

His gaze returned to her. "Like what?"

"John, honestly. I don't know... I mentioned the weather and we talked about the stock market—he was far more knowledgeable about it than I'll ever be. We talked about you, but only a little. Now that you mention it, he did seem nervous at first."

"Avery's always nervous."

"Then there was nothing out of the ordinary."

McFarland sat on the edge of the bed and braced his hands on either side of her head. "It appears I'm in your debt again."

"Good, I like it that way."

He looked as though he wanted to kiss her. He even bent his head closer to hers, his gaze on her lips. Judy wished he would and tried to beckon him with her eyes, but he didn't and left soon afterward, leaving her frustrated and disappointed. He'd kissed her several times since the accident, light kisses that teased her with the memory of other more potent ones. He treated her like...like an indulgent older brother. But she was powerless to change his attitude until she could get out of bed.

Judy crossed her arms and sighed dejectedly. She couldn't blame John for not being tempted by her; she must look a sight in her plain nightgowns. What she wouldn't give for a skimpy piece of silk!

Feeling tired, Judy slept for the next hour and woke to distant hammering, or at least that was what it sounded like.

"What's that noise?" She sat upright, looking at the nurse.

"Is it bothering you? Mr. McFarland instructed me to let him know if the construction disturbed your rest."

"Construction?"

"Yes, Mr. McFarland is having a medical clinic built. I'll be staying on the island full-time following your recovery."

"He's building a clinic?"

"Yes, I've already seen several of the children for physical exams. Arrangements are being made to fly in a doctor twice a week from now on."

Judy was too astonished to make a sound. Grimacing at the pain, she tossed aside the sheets and climbed out of bed. She reached for her robe.

"Ms. Lovin, what are you doing?"

She tried to speak, but couldn't. Instead, she shook her head and walked out of the room.

"Just where do you think you're going?" Virginia Reinholt demanded, hands on her hips.

It was all Judy could do to point down the stairs.

"Ms. Lovin, I must insist that you return to your room immediately. Mr. McFarland will be displeased."

Judy ignored her and carefully moved down the stairs, taking one step at a time. It hurt to walk, but she discovered that pressing her arm against her sides lessened the pain.

The middle-aged nurse ran ahead of Judy and was waiting for her at the bottom of the stairs. "Please—go back to your room this instant."

"No," Judy said with as much resolve as she could muster.

"Then you leave me no option but to inform my employer." The nurse marched toward McFarland's suite of offices.

The flustered woman was standing in front of Avery's desk, visibly distressed, when Judy appeared. Avery wiped his forehead with his handkerchief, straightened his bow tie and nodded now and then.

Judy sidestepped them both, knocked politely on John's door and let herself into his office.

"Judy?" He rose to his feet. "What are you trying to do? Kill yourself?"

He noted her tears and lowered his voice sufficiently. "My Beauty, what is it?" He walked around his desk and pulled her into his arms.

Judy tried to tell him, but her voice refused to cooperate. Whimpering softly, she framed his face with her hands and spread kisses over his jaw and cheeks. Quick, random kisses. She found his eyes, his nose, his ear. She kissed him again and again, ignoring his faint protests.

"Judy," he said thickly, his hands on her upper arms.

He continued to speak, but Judy cut him off by placing her mouth over his, thanking him silently for his thoughtfulness.

The intensity of the kiss rocked them both and, feeling weak, he backed into a chair and sat with her nestled in his lap.

He drew her closer and teased her

with feathery strokes of his tongue. Judy moaned, lost in the sensations.

McFarland had restrained himself from holding or touching her like this. Her innocence humbled him, and he was afraid he'd frighten her with the fierce passion she aroused in him.

Since the accident, he'd kissed her a handful of times, but each gentle kiss had only created more need than it satisfied. Now his desire for her mounted with such intensity that it sapped the strength from him. Emotions that had been hiding just below the surface gushed forth, nearly overpowering him with their intensity.

Groaning, McFarland tore his mouth away and nuzzled his face in her neck, holding her as close as he dared, afraid of causing her further pain. Her tenderness enveloped him, and with it a desire so overwhelming that he couldn't hold her much longer and remain sane.

"John," she pleaded, "don't stop."

He kissed her again because refusing her anything was beyond him. His mouth claimed hers, and when he'd finished, their breathing was labored.

He held her face and wiped the tears from her cheek with the side of his thumb, still aghast at the power she held over him. "What happened?"

She shook her head. "I heard pounding...or what I thought was...pounding."

McFarland nodded, encouraging her to continue.

"You're building a medical clinic?"

"Yes."

She drew her hands over his face, stroking, loving every inch of his features while she gathered her composure. "Thank you," she said in a small voice.

McFarland studied her, more perplexed than ever. He'd given her a host of gifts, but nothing had evoked this response. Not even the sculpture. A simple medical clinic had reduced her to tears.

A loud knock forced them apart.

"I apologize for this rude interruption, Mr. McFarland," the nurse said, standing just inside the door. "There was no stopping her—I did try."

"I flew the coop," Judy whispered and was rewarded with a quick smile from John.

"I really have to insist that she return to bed immediately."

"Oh, do I have to?" Judy asked with a ragged sigh.

McFarland stood, bringing Judy with him. "Yes, you do."

"Another day of this, and you might as well bury me in my nightgown." Playfully, she pressed the back of her hand to her forehead and rolled her eyes.

"Another kiss like that," McFarland said, low enough for only Judy to hear, "and you can bury me, too."

John scooped her into his arms, carrying her up the stairs. Virginia Reinholt led the way back to Judy's room, clucking as she went, listing Judy's myriad transgressions with every step.

McFarland followed Ms. Reinholt into the room and lowered Judy to the bed. She didn't release her arms from around his neck, but held him a moment longer while she whispered, "Just wait until you get sick!"

"Are you sure you're up to this?" McFarland asked for the fifth time in as many minutes. The thought of her on another horse made him wince.

"If you ask me that once more I think I'll scream," Judy told him with a scathing look that added credence to her threat. "It's been three weeks since the accident. I'm not recovering from brain surgery, you know!"

"But horseback riding…"

"If Ms. Reinholt approved, so should you. Besides, I want to ride again before I lose my nerve."

"Never mind yours," McFarland muttered. "Mine's completely shot."

Sam brought both Princess and Midnight to the front of the stables and held Princess while Judy slipped her foot into the stirrup and mounted the mare.

The movement caused a painful twinge, but nothing she couldn't readily disguise. "There," she said triumphantly.

"Right." McFarland swung himself onto Midnight and circled the yard. Judy hadn't fooled him; she was hurting and he was furious that she wouldn't put this off until she'd had time to heal completely.

"Are you coming or not?" She threw the question over her shoulder as she trotted ahead of him toward the beach.

"Judy, slow down!" he shouted, racing after her.

"No."

The wind carried her laughter and McFarland relaxed in his saddle, smiling as the sound washed over him. The last few weeks had drastically altered their relationship.

He'd never spent time like this with a woman. A shared look could have more meaning than an hour's conversation; a kiss in the moonlight could fill him with longing. She might have been innocent, but she aroused in him a sensual awareness far stronger than anything he'd ever known. When she laughed, he laughed; when she ached, he ached; when she was happy, he was happy.

He spent as much of his day with

her as his business would allow. For the first time, he delegated his duties freely. He'd always known that Avery Anderson was a competent manager, but in the past three weeks, he'd learned to fully utilize and appreciate the man's talents.

If McFarland needed to read over papers regarding his business interests, he'd often do it in the evenings. Content simply to be at his side, Judy would sit across from him in the library reading, a book propped open in front of her, while he handled his affairs. Often he found his interest wavering. Watching her was by far the greater joy.

There'd been a time when he was reluctant to take an hour off; now he dedicated whole days to Judy. He couldn't imagine his life without her. Some inner part of himself must have known this would happen—that was the only possible explanation for the fact that he'd forced her to come to the island. For the very first time in his life he was utterly content. There were no more mountains to conquer, no more bridges to cross. There was nothing he desired more than what he possessed at that moment.

"I've missed riding," Judy said happily, breaking into his thoughts.

He'd ridden only five or six times himself, preferring to spend any free hours with her.

"John," she said, her voice softening, "I thought I asked you to stop buying me gifts."

"I vaguely recall something to that effect," he said glibly.

"If you think you've fooled me, you're wrong. I know exactly what's going on."

"I wouldn't dream of disregarding

your wishes." He did his best to disguise a smile.

"I suppose you don't think I've noticed the way Sam's been walking around like a peacock. You've bought another horse."

Shaking his head, McFarland chuckled. "She's a beauty. You're going to love her."

"Oh, John, honestly. What am I going to do with you?"

Love me. Marry me. Have children with me. Fill my life with joy. The possibilities were endless.

"John, look," Judy cried. "The kids are playing in the surf."

McFarland paused, watched their antics and laughed.

"They haven't seen you in a couple of weeks," he said. "Go and talk to them. I'll wait for you here."

"Wait for me?" She turned questioning eyes to him.

"I'll frighten them away."

Judy frowned. She understood what he meant, but it was time the children got to know him the way she did, the way he really was. "But you're with me," she said, climbing down from Princess. "Come on." She held out her hand to him.

McFarland felt a twinge of nervousness as he joined her. He hadn't been around children much and if he admitted the truth, he felt as apprehensive as they did.

"Philippe. Elizabeth." Judy called their names and watched as they turned, then raced toward her.

"Judy!"

Arms went flying around her amid a chorus of happy cries.

Judy fell to her knees and joyously hugged each one.

"We heard you nearly died!"

"There's a nurse on the island now. Did you know that?"

"Paulo got a new tooth."

"It'd take more than a fall to do me in," she told them with a light laugh, dismissing their concern. She lifted her eyes to John's, daring him to contradict her. "Children, I have someone I want you to meet." She rose to her feet and slid her arm around John's waist. "This is Mr. McFarland. He owns the island."

All the children froze until Elizabeth and Margaret curtsied formally, their young faces serious as they confronted John McFarland. The boys bowed.

McFarland frowned, raised his brows at Judy and followed the boys' example, bending low. "I'm pleased to make your acquaintance."

"Did you build us the school?"

"The nurse stuck a needle in my arm, but I didn't cry."

"The doctor said I have to eat my vegetables."

The flurry of activity took him by surprise. Patiently, he was introduced to each child.

"Judy. Judy." Jimmy came running from the edge of the jungle, carrying a huge cage. "Did you see my bird?"

He was so obviously proud of his catch that Judy paid a great deal of attention to the large blue parrot. "Oh, he's lovely."

"I caught him myself," Jimmy went on to explain. "He was trapped in the brush and I grabbed him and put him inside the cage."

The square box had been woven from palm leaves. "You did an excellent job."

"He sings, too. Every morning."

"I think you should set him free," Margaret said, slipping her hand into Judy's. "No one's happy in a cage."

"But he sings," Jimmy countered.

"He's such a pretty bird," Philippe said, sticking his fingers into the holes of the cage. The parrot's wings fluttered madly in an effort to escape.

"I give him food. He'll even let me hold him."

"But how do you know he's happy?" Margaret persisted.

"Because I just do!"

"But how do you know he'll be happy tomorrow?"

"Because he will!"

Judy felt the blood drain from her face. The chatter of the children abated. Even the ocean appeared to hold back the surf. Judy couldn't take her eyes off the parrot, and her throat clogged with emotion. She was like that bird. She'd been coerced into coming here. John had forced her to leave everything she loved behind. He'd given her gift after gift, admired her, held her in high regard, but it had changed nothing. She was still in a cage, a gilded one, but nevertheless a cage. She could flutter her wings, trying to escape, but she was trapped as effectively as the parrot.

"I...think I should get back to the house," she said, her voice shaky.

"It was too much for you." John took her by the elbow and led her over to Princess. "You've gone pale," he told her.

Judy felt as though someone had robbed her of her happiness. Seeing the bird brought her own situation into clear focus. She'd been playing a fool's game to believe she could ever be more than a plaything to John. He'd told her when she first arrived that she'd been brought to St. Steven's to amuse him. She'd fulfilled that expectation well, so content was she with her surroundings.

The ride back to the house seemed to require all her energy.

"I'm contacting the doctor," McFarland announced the minute they'd dismounted and the horses had been led away. "I knew it was too soon, but I went against my better judgment."

"No," Judy said, hardly able to look at him. "I'll go lie down for a moment. Then I'll be fine." That wasn't true, but she needed an excuse to get away from him and think.

A letter was waiting for her on the dresser in her room. She stared at the familiar handwriting and felt overwhelmingly homesick. Tears burned for release as she held the envelope and closed her eyes. Home. Her father. David. New York had never seemed so far from her, or so unattainable.

The content of the letter had a curious effect on her. Suddenly in control of herself again, she marched out of her room and down the stairs.

John was in his office dictating a memo to Avery when she approached him. He looked up, obviously surprised to see her standing here. "Judy," he said softly. "Are you feeling better?"

"I'm fine." She noticed how blithely he smiled, unaware of the change in her. "John, I need to talk to you."

He dismissed Avery with a shake of his head. Judy closed the door after his assistant and turned to face him, pressing her hands against the door. Her lack of emotion astonished even her.

"There was a letter from my family in my room when I returned."

"I'd heard one had been delivered."

She dropped her hands to her side. "My brother's getting married."

"Good." McFarland smiled. "It seems the shipping business has improved." With a little subtle help from him. The Lovins need never know, and it eased his conscience to repay them in some small measure for sending Judy to him.

"My father is thrilled with his choice and so am I. David has loved Marie for several years, but delayed the wedding because...well, you know why."

For having received such good news, Judy didn't appear very happy.

"John," she said, boldly meeting his gaze. "I've been here for nearly three months now."

"Yes."

"You asked me and I came without question. I've never asked to leave."

A sense of dread filled McFarland. "What are you saying?"

"I want to go home."

Nine

"I won't let you go," McFarland said.

Judy closed her eyes at the bitter-sweet pain. "I haven't amused you enough?" At his blank stare, she continued. "That was the reason you brought me to the island, or so you claimed."

"That has nothing to do with it."

"Then what does?"

McFarland's control was slipping and rather than argue, he reached for his pen and scribbled instructions across the top of a sheet. If he ignored her, maybe she would forget her request and drop the matter entirely.

"John," she said, "I'm not leaving this office until you answer me."

"I've already said everything I intend to. The subject is closed."

"The subject is standing in front of you demanding an answer!"

"You're my guest."

"But you won't allow me to leave."

A strained silence fell between them. Judy's breathing was fast and shallow. Her throat burned as she struggled to hold back her emotions.

"John, please."

"You are my guest."

"So I may leave?"

"No!" His rage was palpable. He didn't know why, after all these weeks, she'd ask him to release her. His heart felt like a stone in his chest.

The silence returned.

When Judy spoke again, her voice was soft yet tortured. "Then I'm your prisoner."

She turned and left him, feeling as though she was living out her worst nightmare. She dared not look back; tears threatened but she refused to let them fall.

McFarland watched her go, overcome by an unidentifiable, raw emotion. She called herself his prisoner, but there were chains that bound him just as strongly. She'd come to him and within weeks had altered the course of his life. He couldn't afford to lose Judy—she was his sunshine, his joy. She'd brought summer to the dark winter of his existence. How could he let her go?

Judy returned to her suite, weighed down by grief, sorrow, anger. She'd been happy with John and the island life. Everything had been good—until she'd seen the cage. Until she recognized the bars surrounding her. Perhaps she'd been blinded by her love for him and that was why she'd been able to tolerate this lack of choice, of independence. But now, like the bird wildly seeking escape, her wings were beating frantically, seeking freedom.

She took her brother's letter out of the envelope. For the third time, she read it. Every word was a form of torture. Things she'd taken for granted returned to haunt her. Bently and the funny way he had of speaking out of the corner of his mouth; the dining-room chairs that were a family heritage; the drapes that hung over her bedroom windows.

Her beloved brother was getting married. Some of the weight lifted from her heart as she thought of David as a husband and someday a father. Marie would make him a good wife. His excitement and joy were evident in the letter. She could almost see him with his eyes sparkling and his arm around Marie's shoulder. How Judy wished she could be with him to share in this special moment.

At noon, although she had no appetite, Judy went downstairs, pausing just inside the dining room. John was waiting for her, standing at his end of the table, hands resting on the back of his chair.

"Are you feeling better?" he asked cordially.

"No." She dropped her gaze to the table. A small, beautifully wrapped gift lay beside her water glass. She raised questioning eyes to John. "What's this?"

"Go ahead and open it."

She wanted to tell him that she wouldn't accept any more gifts. He couldn't buy *her* as he'd bought everything else in his life. She wasn't for sale. The only thing she wanted from John McFarland was the freedom to return home, and he wouldn't give her that.

Dutifully, she sat down and peeled away the paper. Inside was a diamond bracelet of such elegance and beauty that she caught her breath. "It's beautiful."

John looked pleased. "I was saving it for just the right moment."

Judy gently closed the velvet box and set it aside. "Why now? Did you want to prove that my shackles are jewel-encrusted? You needn't have bothered, John. I've always known that."

His face convulsed and, as he stared at her, his eyes grew dark and hot.

Neither spoke another word during their meal, and when Judy walked out of the dining room, she pointedly left the bracelet behind.

* * *

A week passed, the longest, most difficult week of Judy's life. She didn't ask John to release her again, but her desire to leave the island hung between them at every meeting. Although she avoided him, he seemed to create excuses to be with her. He chatted easily, telling her little things, pretending nothing had changed. Judy wasn't that good an actress; she spoke only when he asked her a direct question. Although she tried to remain distant and aloof, it was hard.

To work out her frustration, she spent hours riding across the island. The sweltering heat of late summer was oppressive. One afternoon, toward dusk, she changed from her riding clothes into her swimsuit.

The pool was blissfully cool when she dove in. She hoped the refreshing water would alleviate the discomfort of the merciless sun and her own restlessness. She swam lazy laps, drawing comfort from the exercise.

She hadn't been in the water ten minutes when John joined her. As he approached the pool, Judy swam to the shallow end, stood up and shook the wet hair from her face. She defied him with her eyes, demanding that he leave and give her some privacy.

He ignored her silent pleas and jumped into the pool. At first he did a series of laps. Somewhat relieved, Judy continued her exercise. When he suddenly appeared beside her, it was a surprise.

"Remember the last time we were in the water together?" he asked, his voice husky and low.

In an effort to get away from him, Judy swam to the deep end and treaded water. She remembered that afternoon on the beach all too well; he'd held her in his arms while the rolling surf plunged them underwater. He'd kissed her and held her body close to his as the powerful surf tossed them about.

Now his presence trapped her. She refused to meet his look.

"You remember, don't you?" he demanded.

"Yes," she cried, and swallowed hard.

His face tightened and he lowered his voice, each syllable more seductive than the last. "So do I, Judy. I remember the way you slid your arms around my neck and buried your face in my chest."

She shook her head in denial.

"You trembled when I kissed you and you clung to me as though I were your life. I remember everything."

Judy closed her eyes. "Don't," she whispered. She desperately wanted him to leave her.

"I'm not going." He saw that her eyes were overly bright and that she was struggling to hold back the tears. "I miss you. I want things to go back to the way they were."

Her chin rose. "They can't," she said, her mouth trembling. "They'll never be the same."

As much as he tried, McFarland couldn't understand what had changed. Why had she all of a sudden asked to return to New York? He'd tried—heaven knew he'd tried—to understand, but she'd made it impossible. In a week, she'd hardly spoken to him. He'd attempted to draw her out, to discover what was troubling her. All she did was look at him with her large, soulful eyes as though she might burst into tears at any moment. After a week, he was losing his patience.

"Why can't they be the same?" he asked.

"I'm your prisoner."

"No, you aren't," he shouted.

"You brought me here as an amusement."

"In the beginning, perhaps, but that's all different now."

"But it isn't," she said flatly. "Nothing is. I'm your prisoner," she repeated.

"But you were happy."

She flinched at the truth. "Yes, for a time I was."

"What changed?"

"The walls," she said in a tormented voice. "I could see the walls of my cell closing in around me."

McFarland had no idea what she was talking about. Walls? Cell? She had more freedom now than she realized. She ruled his heart; he was hers to do with as she wished.

"Judy," he said, trapping her against the bright blue tile of the pool. His face was only inches from hers. "You're talking nonsense."

"To you, maybe. You don't understand."

"I understand this," he said, weaving his fingers into her wet hair. He kissed her then, pressing his body against her own as he hungrily claimed her mouth.

Judy pulled away, and he didn't stop her. But he said, "It was good with us. You can't have forgotten how good."

"Yes, I remember," she wept. Instinctively, her body arched toward him and she slipped her arms tightly around his neck. She was trembling when he kissed her once more and when she arched against him, he nearly lost his grip on the pool's edge.

"I can't let you go," he whispered. He kissed her gently, slowly, again and again until she was weak and clinging in his arms. His body burned with need for her. Raising his head, he looked into her eyes. "I'll give you anything."

Tears scorched a trail down her face. "I only want one thing."

Knowing what she was about to say, McFarland closed his eyes to the pain.

"I want my freedom," she sobbed. Her shoulders shook uncontrollably as she climbed out of the pool. "I want to go home."

Guilt tore at him. He could deal with anything but her pain. Judy was using his conscience against him and in that moment, McFarland thought he hated her.

Then, seeing her tear-streaked face as she reached for the towel, McFarland realized something more—he hated himself twice as much.

Her tears didn't diminish, even when Judy returned to her room. She was shocked by the power John had to bend her will to his. How easily he'd manipulated her. She had to admit that his kisses were even more potent than her desire to go home to her family. Within minutes she'd been willing to give him anything he wanted.

When McFarland returned to his office, his mood was dark. He was short-tempered with anyone who had the misfortune of being within earshot. It was as though he wanted to punish the world for trying to take away the only woman he'd ever cared about.

"Mr. McFarland," Avery said, late that same afternoon. He stood in the doorway, not daring to approach his employer's desk.

"What is it?" McFarland barked. "I haven't got all day."

"It's Ms. Lovin, sir."

The pencil McFarland was holding snapped in half. "She's staying, Avery, and there's not a damn thing you can say that'll change my mind."

"But her family…"

"What about them?"

"They've personally appealed for your mercy. It seems the Lovin boy is getting married and requests his sister's presence at the wedding."

"They appealed for mercy! I hope you told them I have none." McFarland shuffled through some papers, paying unnecessary attention to them.

"The family's requesting some indication of when you plan to release Ms. Lovin. The wedding can be delayed at…at your convenience."

"Mine." He snickered loudly. "I hope you told them I don't plan to release her." He couldn't explain to Avery that he was *afraid* to release her. Afraid to lose her. Afraid she wouldn't come back.

"You won't let her off the island even to attend her brother's wedding?"

"No."

"But, sir…"

"That will be all, Avery."

McFarland's assistant took a deep breath, as though gathering his courage before speaking.

"Listen, Avery," McFarland said, unwilling to listen to anyone's opinion regarding Judy. His mind was made up. "Feel free to submit your resignation again. Only next time I may not be so willing to give it back."

That evening, McFarland sat alone in the library. During the years he'd been on the island, he'd spent countless nights in this room. Now it felt as cold and unwelcoming as an unmarked grave. When he couldn't tolerate it any longer, he rose and stepped outside, heading toward the stables. A beer with Sam would relax him. He was halfway there when he saw Judy, silhouetted in the moonlight, sitting on the patio by the pool. Her head was slightly bowed, the soft folds of her summer dress pleated around her. The pale light of the moon shone like a halo around her.

The scene affected him more than all her pleas. He remembered standing on the ridge, watching her play with the island children on the beach below. He recalled how her eyes would light up just before his mouth met hers; he recalled how she clung to him. With vivid clarity, he remembered the fall from the horse and how he would've given everything he owned not to see her hurt, not to lose her. Now, he was losing her anyway.

His presence must have disturbed her, because she turned and her eyes found his. McFarland's stomach knotted at the doubt and uncertainty he saw in her gaze. He yearned with everything in him to ease her pain, but if he did he would only increase his own. He needed her. The beast who'd once claimed he needed no one was dependent upon a woman. *This woman*.

The sudden thunder and lightning barely registered in McFarland's mind. The drenching rain soaked him in minutes, and still he didn't move.

Judy came to him, her gaze concerned.

"Go inside," he rasped.

Her face was bloodless. "Not without you."

He nearly laughed. It shouldn't matter to her what became of him; she was the one who wanted to walk out of his life.

"John." She urged him again a moment later.

"I find your solicitude unconvincing."

The flatness of his voice sent a chill through her veins. Judy hesitated.

He saw that she was as drenched as he was. "Go inside," he murmured. "I'll be there in a few minutes."

"If you stay out here, you'll catch a chill."

Raw emotion fueled his anger and he shouted loudly enough to be heard over the furious clap of thunder. "Leave me!"

Her eyes welled with tears.

McFarland couldn't *bear* to see her cry. He stepped close and cupped her face. His heart ached with all the emotion he felt for her. He could *make* her stay, force her to live on the island and ignore her desire to leave. In time she'd forget her family, he told himself, accept her position on St. Steven's and in his life. He would give her everything a woman would possibly want; everything he owned would be hers.

In that moment, McFarland knew that everything he possessed, all his wealth, all that he was, would never be enough for Judy. He dropped his hands and turned toward the house.

When they reached the front door, John opened it for her. Judy paused and looked up at him. Her own distress hardly compared to the misery she witnessed in his eyes.

"John," she whispered brokenly. Even now his unhappiness greatly affected her. Even now she loved him. "I—"

His face tightened as a dark mask descended over his features, a mask she recognized. He'd worn it often in the first weeks after her arrival. She'd forgotten how cold and cruel he could look, how ruthless he could be.

"Don't say it," he interrupted harshly.

"Don't say a single thing. Not a word." He turned and abruptly left her standing alone.

Princess was saddled and ready for Judy early the next morning. She hadn't slept well and looked forward to the rigorous exercise.

"Morning, Sam," she said, without much enthusiasm.

The groom ignored her, holding a gelding's hoof in his lap and running a file across the underside.

"Sam?"

"Morning," he grunted, not looking at her.

"Is something wrong?" Sam had been her ally and friend from the beginning.

"Wrong?" he repeated. "What could be wrong?"

"I don't know."

"For nearly two weeks now, this place has been like a battlefield."

Judy opened her mouth to deny it.

"But does ol' Sam question it? No." He lifted his head to glare at her. "I figured whatever was wrong would right itself in time. Looks like I was wrong."

"I wish it was that simple," Judy murmured, stroking Princess's neck.

Sam continued to file the gelding's hoof. "McFarland bites my head off and you walk around looking like you spent half the night crying your eyes out. You get any paler, and someone could mistake you for a ghost!"

Judy raised her hands to her cheeks, embarrassed.

Sam lowered the horse's leg to the ground and slowly straightened. "Mc-Farland been shouting at you again?"

"No."

"Has he been unfair?"

"That's not what this is about."

"Did he get after you for something you didn't do?"

"No."

Hands on his hips, Sam took a step toward her. "Do you love him or not?"

Judy felt the blood rush through her veins.

"Well?" he demanded.

"Yes," she answered, her voice shaking uncontrollably.

"I thought so."

She pushed back her hair. "Loving someone doesn't fix everything."

"Then do whatever you have to do to make it right."

Judy swallowed down the hard lump that had formed in her throat. Sam made everything sound so...uncomplicated.

"For heaven's sake, woman, put an end to this infernal bickering. And do it soon, while there's still a man or woman who's willing to work for John McFarland."

Judy rode for hours. When she returned, a maid announced that McFarland wished to see her at her earliest convenience. With her heart pounding, Judy rushed upstairs for a quick shower.

By the time she appeared in John's office Avery seemed greatly relieved to see her.

"You're to go right in," he instructed.

"Thank you, Avery," she said as he opened the door.

John was writing, his head bent, and although she was fairly sure he knew she was there, he chose to ignore her.

After the longest minute of her life, he looked up at her and gestured for her to take a seat. His expression was cool and distant.

Judy shivered as she sat down. "I've

been in communication with New York this morning," he said evenly.

She nodded, not knowing what he was leading up to. He could be referring to her family, but he hadn't said as much.

"The launch will leave the island at five tomorrow morning. However, the helicopter is at your disposal."

Judy blinked. "Are you saying I'm free to go?"

"That's exactly what I'm saying."

It took a moment for the full realization to hit her. She sighed as the burden was lifted from her shoulders. "John—"

He interrupted her. "From what I understand, you'll be home in plenty of time for your brother's wedding."

Her smile was tremulous. "Thank you."

He nodded abruptly. "Is tomorrow soon enough, or would you prefer to leave now?"

"Tomorrow is fine."

He returned to his paperwork.

"John..."

"If you'll excuse me, I have work to do," he said pointedly.

Judy stood, clasping her fingers tightly in front of her. "I'll never forget you, John McFarland, or this island."

He continued with his work as though she hadn't spoken.

"If I don't see you again..."

John glanced at his watch and while she was speaking, reached for his phone.

Judy blinked back stinging tears of anger and embarrassment.

"Goodbye, John," she said softly, and with great dignity, turned and left his office.

That evening Judy ate alone. The dining-room table had never seemed so big or the room so empty. She'd spent the afternoon preparing for her departure. Her suitcase was packed, her room bare of the things that had marked it as hers. She'd visited the children one last time and stopped at the stables to feed Princess and Midnight. Sam had grumbled disapprovingly when he heard she was leaving and when she hugged him goodbye, the gruff old man's eyes glistened.

After all the excitement, Judy had expected to sleep that evening. To her surprise, she couldn't.

At midnight, she made her way down the stairs for a glass of milk. She noticed light from under the library door and cracked it open to investigate. She found John sitting at the oak desk, a half-full whiskey bottle in one hand and a shot glass in the other.

He raised his head to study her when she entered the room, and his eyes narrowed. "What are you doing here?"

The words were slurred. Judy shook her head, hardly able to believe what she was seeing. In all the weeks that she'd been on the island, John had never abused alcohol. "You're drunk."

He lifted the bottle in mocking salute. "You're darn right I am."

"Oh, John." She nervously tucked her hair behind her ears, feeling wretched.

"You think too highly of yourself if you assume I did this because you're leaving."

"I..."

He refilled his glass, the whiskey sloshing over the sides. He downed the contents in one swallow and glared at her. "You were a nuisance."

Judy didn't respond.

"I should've got rid of you weeks ago."

Ten excellent reasons to walk away presented themselves. Judy ignored each one. For some perverse reason she wanted to hear what he had to say.

"You're such a goody-goody."

She clasped her fingers more tightly together.

"I could've had you several times. You know that, don't you? You were willing enough." His eyes challenged her to defy him. "But I didn't take what you so generously offered." His short laugh was without humor. He leaned forward and glared at her. "You know why? I like my women hot and spicy. You're sweet, but you'd soon grow tasteless."

Judy's face burned with humiliation; each word was like a lash across her back.

His eyes were cold. "Why are you still standing there?"

Unable to answer him, Judy shook her head.

"Get out!" he roared. "Out of my house! Out of my life!"

Part of Judy yearned to wrap her arms around him and absorb his anger and his pain. But she didn't move, didn't take a step forward.

"Go on," he shouted. "Get out of here before I do something we'll both regret."

"Goodbye, John," she whispered. She closed the massive doors when she left and flinched at the unexpected sound of breaking glass.

"Goodbye, Beauty."

The words were so faint that Judy wasn't sure she'd heard them.

Judy sat in her room, waiting for the sun to rise. She hadn't slept after the confrontation in the library; she hadn't even tried.

At four, the maid came to wake her and was surprised to find her already up. "Mr. Anderson will escort you to the dock," the girl informed her.

"Thank you."

Avery was waiting for Judy at the bottom of the stairs. He took the suitcase from her hand and gave her a sympathetic smile. Judy paused and glanced in the direction of the library.

"Take care of him for me, will you?" she asked.

Avery cleared his throat and looked doubtful. "I'll do my best."

The launch was at the dock. Judy hugged John's assistant and Sam, who arrived at the last minute, looking flustered and upset.

Only when the boat had sped away did Judy turn back to the island. In the distance she saw a third figure standing separate from the others.

John McFarland watched the only woman he'd ever loved vanish from his life. In releasing her, he had made the ultimate sacrifice. It was probably the one completely unselfish act of his lonely life.

Ten

The sound was what astonished Judy most. Street noise: buses, taxis, traffic, shouts, raised voices, laughter, televisions, radios. The clamor was less irritating than it was distracting. The island had taught her to appreciate the wonders of silence.

But this was Manhattan, not St. Steven's Island, Judy had to repeatedly remind herself. The first few days after her arrival home, she'd felt as though she'd returned to another planet.

The life that had once been familiar
and comfortable felt strangely out of
sync—and appallingly loud. In time,
she knew she'd adjust, just as she'd
adapted to life on the island.

"It's McFarland, isn't it?" her father
asked her over breakfast the first week
she was home.

"John?"

Charles Lovin's features were tight
with anxiety. The months apart had
taken their toll on him. It showed in
the way his eyes followed her, his gaze
sad and troubled. "McFarland treated
you abominably, didn't he?"

"Of course not," Judy answered, dismissing her father's fears with a generous smile. "John McFarland was the
perfect gentleman."

"From the beginning?"

Judy lowered her eyes to her plate as
a twinge of loneliness brought tears to

her eyes. "In his own way, yes. He's an unusual person."

"You think I don't know that? I died a thousand deaths worrying about you alone with that...that beast."

"I wasn't alone with John and, Father, really, he isn't a beast."

Charles Lovin's instant denial faded in Judy's ears. She pretended to be listening while her father listed John's many faults in a loud, haranguing voice. Her thoughts were a thousand miles away on a Caribbean island where orchids grew in abundance and children laughed and a man ruled his own kingdom.

"Judy, are you listening to me? Judy?"

"I'm sorry," she said contritely, looking at her father. "What were you saying?"

Father and son exchanged meaningful glances.

"I'm sure you can appreciate that Dad and I were concerned about you," David said, studying his sister.

"Naturally. I would've been worried myself had the circumstances been reversed," Judy murmured, feeling wretched. She wanted to defend John, but both her father and her brother were filled with bitterness toward him.

"He never spoke to us personally," David continued. "I can't begin to tell you how frustrated Dad and I were. We must've contacted McFarland a hundred times and never got past that assistant of his. By the way, what's this Anderson fellow like?"

"Avery?"

"Yes. I tell you, he's an expert at sidestepping questions. No matter how much Dad and I hounded him, we never got a straight answer."

At the memory of Avery Anderson, Judy brightened and spent the next five minutes describing John's assistant. "He really is a funny little man. So polite and—"

"Polite!" Her father nearly choked on his coffee. "The next thing I know, you'll be telling me McFarland's a saint."

Judy blushed at the memory of the times he could have made love to her, and hadn't. "In some ways he *was* a saint."

Her announcement was followed by a stunned silence.

"Any man who pulls the kind of stunts John McFarland does will burn in hell," Charles Lovin stated emphatically.

"Father!"

"I mean it. That man is a demon."

Judy pushed her plate aside and managed not to defend John. "And just what did he do that was so terrible?"

"Why, he…he nearly destroyed our business."

"It's thriving now. You told me so yourself."

"Now!" Charles Lovin spat. "But McFarland drove us to the brink of disaster, then took delight in toying with us."

"He told me once that he held you in high regard," Judy informed him.

"Then Lord help us if he ever wants to be my friend!"

With great difficulty, Judy kept her own counsel. Neither her father nor her brother understood John the way she did. In their position, she'd probably feel differently, but that didn't change her opinion of him, her love for him.

"Does he do this sort of thing often?" David asked, as he sliced his ham.

Judy blinked, not understanding.

"Were there other women on the island?" he elaborated.

"A few. But I was the only one he…" She paused and searched for the right word.

"You were the only woman he black-mailed into coming?" her father finished for her.

"The only one he sent for," Judy corrected calmly.

"That man is a menace to society," Charles muttered angrily as he sipped his coffee.

Judy couldn't tolerate their insults any longer. She sighed and shook her head. "I hate to disappoint you both, but John McFarland is kind and good. He treated me with respect the entire time I was on the island."

"He held you like a prisoner of war."

"He released me when I asked," she told them, stretching the truth only a bit.

"He did?"

"Of course." She dabbed the corner

of her mouth with her napkin, ignoring the way both men were staring at her.

"He held you for three months, Judy," David said, watching her keenly. "You mean to say in all that time you never asked to leave?"

"That's right."

Again father and son exchanged looks.

"I don't expect you to understand," she told them lamely. "The island is a tropical paradise. I didn't think of asking to leave until…until the end."

The dining room grew silent.

Her father hugged Judy before she left. "It's good to have you home, Beauty."

"It's good to be home, Dad."

In her bedroom, Judy ran her fingers over the brocade-covered headboard and experienced none of the homecoming sensations she'd expected. She loved this room; it was part of her youth, part of her existence before she'd met John McFarland.

Sitting on her bed, Judy felt a poignant sense of loss. She'd changed on the island. Because of John, she'd learned what it was to be a woman and no matter how much she might have wished otherwise, she couldn't go back to being the frightened girl who'd left New York.

A letdown was only natural, Judy tried to reason with herself. When she'd been on the island, home had seemed ideal. Everything was perfect in New York. There were no problems, no difficulties, no heartache. To her dismay, she'd discovered that reality falls far short of memory....

A polite knock at the door diverted her attention from her troubled thoughts. "Come in."

Marie Ashley, David's fiancée,

walked into the room. "Are you ready?"

"I've been ready for weeks," Judy said, rising from the bed. She slipped on a pair of comfortable shoes. "I plan to shop till I drop."

"Me, too," Marie said, her eyes shining. "David and I need so many things. Oh, Judy, we're going to be so happy." She hugged her arms around her middle and sighed with ecstasy. "Did he tell you that I broke into tears when he proposed? I couldn't even answer him. Poor David, I'm sure he didn't know what to make of me, blubbering and carrying on like that."

"I imagine he got the message when you threw your arms around his neck and started kissing him."

Marie's hands flew to her hips. "He told you!"

"Ten times the first day I was home," Judy told her cheerfully. "I don't know who's more excited, you or my brother."

"Me," Marie said unequivocally.

Laughing, they hurried down the stairs to the sports car Marie had parked out front.

The day was a busy one. True to their word, both women shopped until their feet ached and they couldn't carry another package. They ended up back at the Lovin family home, bringing takeout Chinese food for dinner.

Judy deposited her shopping bags in the polished entryway. "Bently," she called, "we're home."

A quick grin cracked the butler's stiff facade as he regarded the pair of them. He already treated Marie like a family member. "Several wedding gifts arrived this afternoon," he informed them primly.

"Here?" Marie asked, surprised.

"I can assure you, Miss Ashley, I

did not haul them from your family's home."

"Where are they, Bently?" Judy asked, sharing a smile with Marie.

"In the library."

"Come on," Marie said eagerly, "let's go check out the loot."

Judy followed her soon-to-be sister-in-law into the book-lined room.

"I took the liberty of unwrapping them for you," Bently said.

Judy and Marie paused in the doorway and gasped at the rich display of paintings and sculptures. Judy's hand flew to her heart. Each piece was lovingly familiar; they were the things her father had sold in a desperate attempt to save the shipping line. The ones he'd surrendered piece by piece, prolonging the agony.

"All this?" Marie breathed. "Who? Who would possibly give us so much?"

Judy knew the answer even before Bently spoke.

"The card says John McFarland."

Judy's eyes drifted shut. John, her John.

"Why, he's the man—" Marie stopped short. "Judy?" Her voice was low and hesitant. "Are you all right?"

Judy opened her eyes. "Of course. Why shouldn't I be?"

"You look like you're about to faint."

"It's from lack of nourishment," Judy explained, her voice shaking. "You dragged me through half the department stores in Manhattan and didn't feed me lunch. What do you expect?"

"I want you to tell me everything. Now sit down."

Judy did because she wasn't convinced she could remain upright for much longer.

"Bently, bring us some coffee, please."

"Right away, Miss Ashley."

Despite her misery, Judy smiled, finding a new respect for her brother's fiancée. "I swear, within a year you'll be the one running the family business."

"I'll have my hands full managing David," Marie returned matter-of-factly.

The coffee arrived and Marie poured, handing Judy the first cup. "You don't need to say much," she began. "It's obvious to me that you love him."

Judy dropped her gaze. "I do. Unfortunately, my family hates him. They think he's some kind of monster."

"But you know better?"

"I do, Marie. He frightened me in the beginning—he can be terrifying. Believe me, I know he's arrogant and stubborn, but as the weeks passed, I discovered that underneath he's a man like every other man. One with hurts and doubts and fears. I learned how kind and generous he can be."

"But, Judy, he forced you to live on that island."

"It's beautiful there. Paradise."

"David and your father thought he was mistreating you."

"Never. Not intentionally. Once I had a riding accident—my fault, actually, although John seemed to blame himself and—"

Marie gasped.

"I didn't let my family know," Judy said. "They would only have worried and I couldn't see any point in increasing their anxiety."

"What happened?"

"I fell—it doesn't matter. What does matter is that John was so wonderful to me. I've never seen anyone more concerned. He spent hours taking care of me. I think he slept in my room for at least two nights. Every time I woke up, he was there. I...I didn't know any man could be so gentle."

Marie smiled faintly. "What are you planning to do now?"

Judy held the coffee cup with both hands. "I...don't know."

"Do you want to go back to the island?"

Judy hung her head and whispered, "Yes. Nothing's the same without John. I loved St. Steven's, but more important, I love John."

"Oh, Judy, your father..."

"I know." She managed to keep her voice steady. "I think he'd rather die than see me go back to the island. John will always be the beast in his eyes."

"Give him time," Marie suggested. "Look what happened with David and me."

Judy wasn't sure she understood. "I know David hasn't seen anyone but you for a couple of years."

"Five years, Judy. I waited five long years for that man."

Judy had no idea the romance between them had been going on all that time.

"Because of the financial problems with the business, David told me it could be years before he'd be in a position to marry me or anyone. He said it was useless for me to wait."

"How painful for you."

"Oh, it gets worse. He broke off our relationship and suggested I marry someone else. When I refused, he insisted I start seeing other men. He made a point of introducing me to his friends and when that didn't work..." Her eyes were dull with pain.

"What happened?"

"I wouldn't give up on him. I loved him too much. If he didn't want to marry me, then I wasn't getting married. There's never been anyone else for me. Only David."

"What did he do?"

Marie's smile revealed a great sadness. "He said some cruel things in an effort to keep me from what he called wasting my life."

Judy recalled her last night on the island and the horrible things John had said to her. He loved her; she was sure of it. But he'd never asked her to stay, never *told* her he loved her. Still, she knew he did....

"Of course, all his insults didn't work," Marie continued. "I knew what he was doing. But he couldn't have gotten rid of me to save his soul."

"I take it he tried."

Marie's mouth quivered. "Oh, yes, for months. Inventive schemes, too, I might add, but I'm more stubborn than he took into account."

Judy gripped her friend's hand. "I hope he knows how lucky he is."

"Are you kidding? I plan to remind him every day for the next fifty years. Now," she said, taking a huge breath, "it's your turn, Judy Lovin, to prove to a man that you mean business."

Judy's gaze rested on their clasped hands. "The night before I left the island, I found John…drinking. He told me he was glad to see me go."

"What did you say?"

"Nothing."

"Good."

"Good?"

"Right. He didn't mean it."

"I know. He was hurting."

Marie smiled. "The guilt's probably driving him crazy about now."

Judy studied her brother's fiancée. "What makes you say that?"

Marie gestured toward the array of

wedding gifts that filled the library. "Look around you."

"But—"

"No buts, girl," Marie interrupted. "You're going back to the island. And when you do he'll be so happy to see you there won't be a single doubt."

Judy went pale.

"It's what you want, isn't it?"

"Yes, but Father and David…"

"Just who are you planning to spend the rest of your life with, anyway? Do you really believe they'll appreciate your sacrifice? Do you think my family was overjoyed with me hanging around year after year?" Marie asked. "Good grief, no! They were convinced that unless I married David, I was going to become a permanent fixture at the old homestead."

Judy laughed, despite her misery.

"My dad was practically bringing home strangers off the street to introduce to me. I'm telling you, between David and my father, I turned down two neurosurgeons, a dentist, three attorneys and a construction tycoon."

The thought was so ridiculous that Judy couldn't stop laughing. Soon Marie joined her and they kept it up until their sides hurt and tears rolled down their faces.

That one talk with her future sister-in-law gave Judy all the fortitude she needed to face an army of Charles Lovins. She chose her moment well— the reception following David and Marie's wedding.

"Father," she said, standing beside him in the receiving line. "I have something to tell you."

He shook hands with a family friend before turning to his daughter. "Yes, Beauty?"

"I love John McFarland."

She expected a bellow of outrage, anger…something other than his acceptance and love. "I suspected as much. Are you going back to him?"

Tears brimmed in Judy's eyes. "Yes."

"When?" His own voice sounded choked.

"Soon."

"He'll marry you?"

Judy chuckled and winked at her sister-in-law. "He'd better."

Charles Lovin arched his eyebrows. "Why's that?"

"I'm not taking no for an answer. Marie and I have a bet on which one of us is going to present you with your first grandchild."

The older man's eyes sparkled with unshed tears. "Then what are you doing sticking around here?" He hugged her fiercely. "Be very, very happy."

"I know I will. You'll come visit?"

"If he'll allow it."

Her arms tightened around him. "He will, I promise."

The launch slowed to a crawl as it approached the dock of St. Steven's Island. Two formidable security guards were waiting to intercept the unannounced intruders.

"Ms. Lovin?"

"Hello, Wilson," Judy said, handing him her luggage. "Is Mr. McFarland available?"

The guard looked uncertain. "I believe he is. Does he know you're coming?"

"No."

He winced at that, but didn't hesitate to help her climb out of the boat.

"Will you see to it that my things are delivered to my room?" Judy asked.

"Right away."

"Thank you, Wilson."

By the time Judy arrived at the

house, there was a small army of Mc-
Farland employees following her, all
talking excitedly.

Sam arrived, breathless from the stables. "Hot dog," he cried and slapped
his knee. "It's about time you got here."

"I was only gone two weeks."

"That's about thirteen days too
long!"

"How has he been?"

Sam rolled his eyes. "Impossible!"

Judy glanced around to see that several of the other employees were nod-
ding their heads, agreeing with Sam's
assessment.

"He's fired me three times in the last
week alone," Wilson volunteered.

"Moi aussi," the chef added, cere-
moniously crossing his arms over his
chest, greatly insulted. "He had ze
nerve to suggest I return to cooking
school."

"Everything will be better now

that Ms. Lovin's here," Sam assured the irate staff. "Next time you leave, though," he warned Judy, "we'll all be on that boat with you."

Ms. Reinholt, who'd stayed to work at the new medical clinic, gave a decisive nod.

"I won't be leaving," Judy told them confidently.

A small cheer arose and when she entered the house, she was met by a red-faced Avery.

"Ms. Lovin!" He looked stunned, flustered, then relieved. "Oh, thank God you're back."

"Where is he?" she asked, resisting the urge to hug her friend.

"The library." He pointed in the direction of the closed doors as though he expected her to have forgotten. "I tried to take care of him like you wanted," Avery said, his words coming out in a rush. "Only, Mr. McFarland, well, he didn't take kindly to my concern."

"I can imagine," Judy said, grateful for such loyal friends.

Summoning her courage, she stood in front of the library doors. She found it fitting that he would be there. The last time she'd confronted him had been in the same room. Only this time, she planned to do all the talking.

She didn't knock, but opened the doors and stepped inside.

"I said I wasn't to be disturbed!" John shouted.

Judy's heart constricted at the sight he made, hunched behind a desk. He looked hard, his blue eyes devoid of any emotion except anger and regret. She noted the lines of fatigue around his eyes and the flatness of his mouth.

"John, it's me," she said softly, loving him so much that only strength of will prevented her from walking into his arms.

His head snapped up. His eyes went wide with questioning disbelief and he half rose from his chair. "Beauty." He froze as though he couldn't decide what to do.

"Don't, John."

"Don't?" he repeated, puzzled.

"Don't ask me to leave. I won't, you know."

McFarland heard the catch in her voice and sank back into the leather chair. How well she knew him; the words had dangled on the tip of his tongue. He'd been about to demand that she go right back where she came from. It wasn't what he wanted, but he had to protect her from himself.

Judy moved farther into the room. "David's wedding was beautiful, and ours is going to be just as special."

"Ours?" he mocked.

"Yes, ours! You're marrying me, John McFarland."

"You're sure taking a lot for granted."

"Perhaps."

"Judy, no." He wiped his face and wondered if he was dreaming. He wasn't. "Don't do this. You're making it difficult to send you away."

She met his eyes boldly. "I plan on making it impossible."

He said nothing for the longest moment. "Judy, there's someone better for you in New York. Some man who'll give you the kind of life you deserve. Some man your father will approve of. He's right—I am a beast."

She planted her hands on his desktop, remembering everything Marie had gone through for David. "I only want *you.*"

"Forcing you to come here, to live on the island, was a mistake."

His face revealed nothing, but she

felt the powerful undertow of his emotions.

"It's not a mistake for me to love you, John."

He flinched as though she'd struck him.

"I'm not good enough for you," he told her in a hard, implacable voice. "The things I did to your family...the things I did to you."

"Coming to this island was right for me. *You're* right for me. I love you. All I ask is that you love me in return."

Again he flinched, and his jaw tensed. He reached out to stroke her cheek. "I've loved you from the moment you showed me how you'd tamed Midnight."

Her gaze holding his, Judy walked around the desk.

McFarland stood.

She slipped her arms around his neck and leaned into him. "Oh, John, life doesn't make sense without you. I had to leave you to learn that. There's no one else for me, no other place I want to be but here."

"Judy." His fingers plowed through her hair as he slanted his mouth over hers. He kissed her again and again, as though it would take a hundred years to make up for these past two weeks.

"I live in a tropical paradise and it was winter without you," he breathed into her hair.

"It's summer now," she whispered.

"Yes," he said, his voice raw. His hand was gentle on her hair. "I love you, Beauty. But I don't know why you'd want to marry a beast."

"I have my reasons," she said as she lovingly pushed him back into his chair. "There's a small wager I need to tell you about."

"Oh?" He pulled her into his lap and

she leaned forward and whispered it in his ear.

The sound of McFarland's laughter drifted through the library doors and the seven who'd gathered there sighed contentedly.

Winter had left the island, never to return.

From that moment, the people of St. Steven's liked to tell how the Beast was gone forever.

Beauty had tamed him.

* * * * *

The
ESSENTIAL COLLECTION

YES! Please send me the *Essential Collection by Debbie Macomber* in Larger Print. This collection begins with 3 FREE books and 2 FREE gifts in the first shipment, and more free gifts will follow! My books will arrive in 8 monthly shipments until I have the entire 51-book *Essential Collection by Debbie Macomber.* I will receive 2 or 3 FREE books in each shipment and I will pay just $4.99 U.S./$5.89 CDN. for each of the other 4 books in each shipment, plus $2.99 for shipping and handling. *If I decide to keep the entire collection, I'll have paid for only 32 books because 19 books are FREE! I understand that by accepting the 3 free books and gifts places me under no obligation to buy anything. I can always return a shipment and cancel at any time. My free books and gifts are mine to keep no matter what I decide.

261 HCN 1446   461 HCN 1446

Name	(PLEASE PRINT)	
Address		Apt. #
City	State/Prov.	Zip/Postal Code

Signature (if under 18, a parent or guardian must sign)

Mail to the **Harlequin® Reader Service:**

IN U.S.A.: P.O. Box 1867, Buffalo, NY 14240-1867
IN CANADA: P.O. Box 609, Fort Erie, Ontario L2A 5X3

* Terms and prices subject to change without notice. Prices do not include applicable taxes. Sales tax applicable in N.Y. Canadian residents will be charged applicable taxes. This offer is limited to one order per household. All orders subject to approval. Credit or debit balances in a customer's account(s) may be offset by any other outstanding balance owed by or to the customer. Please allow 4 to 6 weeks for delivery. Offer available while quantities last. Offer not available to Quebec residents.

EDMBPA14